for my mother, Pam McAlpine

Penguin Books
DOG ROCK

David Foster was born in 1944 and spent his early childhood in Katoomba in the Blue Mountains of New South Wales. He trained as a scientist at Sydney University and the Australian National University and spent 1970 in the United States as a Fellow of the National Institute of Health, and 1978 in Europe as recipient of the Marten Bequest for Prose. His novel *The Pure Land* (1974) shared the first *Age* award for the best Australian book of the year, and his novel *Moonlite* (1981) won the National Book Council Award for Australian Literature. He is married with six children and lives in the southern highlands of New South Wales.

BY THE SAME AUTHOR

North South West
The Pure Land
The Empathy Experiment (with D. Lyall)
Escape to Reality
Moonlite
Plumbum

DOG ROCK

A Postal Pastoral

David Foster

Penguin Books

Published with the assistance of the Literature Board
of the Australia Council

Penguin Books Australia Ltd,
487 Maroondah Highway, P.O. Box 257
Ringwood, Victoria, 3134, Australia
Penguin Books Ltd,
Harmondsworth, Middlesex, England
Penguin Books,
40 West 23rd Street, New York, N.Y. 10010, U.S.A.
Penguin Books Canada Ltd,
2801 John Street, Markham, Ontario, Canada
Penguin Books (N.Z.) Ltd,
182–190 Wairau Road, Auckland 10, New Zealand

First published by Penguin Books Australia, 1985

Typeset in Century Old Style & Franklin Gothic expanded 10% by Dudley E. King, Melbourne

Made and printed in Australia by
The Dominion Press–Hedges & Bell

Foster, David 1944– .
Dog rock.

ISBN 0 14 007652 2.

I. Title.
A823′.3

Acknowledgements

I wish to thank Carl Harrison-Ford and Nicholas Hasluck for helpful suggestions. This book was written with the financial assistance of the Literature Board of the Australia Council.

1 It was ten o'clock on Sunday night when I arrived in Dog Rock so I saw at once the sort of place it was and is.

The streets were deserted. The street lights, singeing the wings of the white Bogong moth, shone down on a town bereft of life except for the flicker on the lounge room curtains in every house of the town, each one of which sounded, despite its size, as though it harboured an auditorium.

I can now state this flicker falls into two discernible patterns, more in the case of those householders who have gone to the height of erecting above the roof of their home one, in some cases two, huge television reception masts. These, with the native ribbon gum and introduced Monterey pine, dominate the town skyline and serve to educate and inform the inhabitants on every matter of national and international importance.

As I passed the steps of my future place of employment, the Post Office, I recalled it was rumoured to be built to the wrong plans, being obviously better suited to a tropical city of some 100,000 residents than a small temperate mountain village of 776. As I have come to know it better, I find I can never enter it without observing its high ceiling and capacious draughty interior, in one corner of which, during the bitter Dog Rock winter, the Postmaster huddles over the bars of a three-bar radiator.

In the bike shed are six wheel-width grooves in the concrete floor, presumably meant for six pushbikes; yet Sambo Fargo and myself, working week about, have ample time to chat on the beat and still get the whole run done in three hours, in the absence of householders, electricity accounts, Christmas cards and *Bowls* magazines.

Of course we are postmen of rare experience, both expert in riding a pushbike before graduating to the motorized variety, and of how many postmen in the Western world today can this be said? But when I say we have the time to chat, I should add I never do: I made it my business to keep myself to myself from the word go, and not entirely through a false sense of superiority: a postman, in the course of his duties, can acquire a good deal of local knowledge, a fact of which I have recently been reminded; but even before I arrived in Dog Rock I resolved to ignore it completely, a decision nothing I have seen or encountered here has made me regret.

Strangely enough this attitude, which in someone else of importance might have incurred the townfolk's displeasure, seems to have won me their approval: I find myself regarded, not as a snob, but as a martyr to my social position, one of the few postmen in Dog Rock history to take his responsibilities seriously.

During the week in which he does not deliver the mail, the Dog Rock postman mans all night the Dog Rock manual telephone exchange, which boasts a twenty-four hour service. One of the last of its kind anywhere, this exchange is housed, for the time being, in a recent cream brick addition to the Post Office, built before Telecom and Australia Post went their separate ways, and meant for the new automatic exchange, which, like a scaffold outside a cell block, is being assembled even now in a room adjacent to the manual exchange and separated from it by a wall completely soundproof. The bifurcation of Postmaster General into Mailmaster and Phonemaster has left, in its wake, my colleague Sambo Fargo and me – D'Arcy D'Oliveres – as perhaps the only evidence of any former central authority; for until the automatic exchange becomes operational we are left, trapped as it were in a time warp, doomed to work for one authority by night and the other by day.

What is worse, one of us will have to go as there is work for one postman only. And neither of us is a young man and Fargo has lived in Dog Rock all his life, through a sense of duty.

A large feature window with pale blue venetian blinds, scrupulously clean, covers most of the southern wall of the exchange but looks out on nothing more picturesque than a high paling fence in good repair, and a few feet further back, the freshly painted rear entrance to Long Wun's Vietnamese restaurant. As the night operator comes on duty at 10 p.m. and leaves at 8 the next morning, the view through this window is of no concern to him. During the day the girls have no time to look out windows, being far too busy coping, at times single-handed, with upwards of 300 subscribers ('subs'), using antique brass jacks connected to cords resembling the distal end of a bicycle pump. This produces, on such occasions as Christmas morning and Mother's Day, a switchboard resembling the wiring diagram of an early valve computer or the mating ball of the Manitoban garter snake.

Not that anyone has ever been heard to complain; on the contrary. On one occasion when the Telecom techs were on strike and refusing to repair equipment, the trunk-line traffic for the whole of Australia was routed through Dog Rock, without apparent delay. Each telephonist received, on the advice of the Governor General, a packet of plum cake mix and a personal commendation.

Fargo and I are as adept as any girl when it comes to handling heavy traffic and on those rare occasions when, for some such reason as bushfire, we are forced to contend with a mass shutter drop, we never become in the least flustered, not a bit of it. Sambo especially is famous for the courteous manner in which he unfailingly greets subscribers, in particular Mrs Topwaite of Ninkum Street, who has a penchant for wishing to speak with her daughter in South Dakota at the oddest of times.

3

And here it is September again and my tenth year in Dog Rock.

September days in Dog Rock can be very warm, but owing to the altitude, nights are invariably cool. Dullard MacLollard, whose memories of frosts seem to stretch back well over a century, makes it his rule never to plant seed potatoes before the first of October; and indeed his crop is always the marvel of the district and a sight to behold.

This very morning I noticed bees moving from the pussy willow to the lavender.

For purposes of orientation I shall now describe a typical Sunday night in the exchange. A week on the exchange, for the night operator, begins Sunday and ends Saturday, and if this seems a trivial point, I must emphasize this is a trivial town, where nothing ever happens which is not essentially trivial.

Until last month when something *quadrivial* happened.

I shall now describe events in the exchange last night, and by extension, what happened in the town. Not that anything happened; just to give some idea of Dog Rock, the sort of place it is.

I shall use the present tense to conceal the thinness of my material.

At 10.02 p.m. I unlock the external door to the exchange. Renee Calvary, a small plump woman in her late thirties who wears her hair in a lacquered beehive, pushes past on her way out.

'Sorry, D'Arce, must run. Very quiet. Two shutters down.'

Renee has brought her husband's car in to work and parked it in the narrow lane next to the incinerator, though her residence, on the opposite side of the railway line in that area of Dog Rock known locally as 'Foggy Hollow', both on account of the low-lying nature of the terrain and the confused state of the inhabitants, who can never be sure whether to spend their money on drink or lottery tickets, is, to use the language of a real estate agent, within five minutes' easy level walking distance. This car, a blue Chevrolet Biscayne, is prone to bound off backwards like a bushwalker confronted with a black snake as soon as the difficult task of finding and engaging its reverse gear has been completed, and so I stand a moment in the doorway – savouring, through both nostrils, the delicate aroma of Renee's perfume – in order to watch this tiny woman's struggles with the transmission of this vast machine. I have been to drive-in theatres in my time and must confess I find a stimulus in such restless front seat activity, accompanied by language growing steadily coarser as Renee's favourite Sunday night television programme ticks by in her absence; and when at last succeeding in her task and holding the brake pedal level with the floor as best she can in her platform heels while at the same time wrestling the fur-covered steering wheel – which seems to spin freely without perceptibly altering the direction the car has moved in – she disappears from my bold gaze past the corner of the Post Office bike shed, it is to my relief; for had she found it necessary to return to the exchange, for whatever reason, there could be no telling what might not have befallen her there.

After she has gone I stand under the hundred-watt bulb till I hear the engine die and the car door slam. Then I go inside.

Woken by the ill-tempered slamming of Renee's car door, Irving Calvary, railway engineman, not a Telecom subscriber, rises from his bed and walks outside the house. He has no doubt as to who's woken him. Concluding that since he is now awake he may as well enjoy a cigarette, he returns briefly to his kitchen, walking gingerly as he passes the door where he invariably sets two fresh saucers of milk for Ginger before retiring. It is not this man's habit to waste electricity, or for that matter anything else, barring milk, and his house might even be thought deserted, as it is also his habit never to return home before dark and always to leave before dawn, whatever the weather and by goods train. He is not known to frequent any club or pub in the district – the district taken to include all that land within the electoral

5

division of D'Entrecasteaux and the subdivision of Hartog and the parish of Ramsdown and its neighbouring parishes Onslow and Offquick – and he is never to be seen reading the evening paper at the grimy window of a passing loco. His garbage bin, of cracked red plastic, stands empty on the grass outside his front gate from one month to the next, until damage sustained in the course of its rolling around the street during the annual spring gales obliges him to replace it with another of red plastic, uncracked, and the only mail he is known to receive, apart from unsolicited householders, is an unsolicited electricity account and an unsolicited annual rates notice – first notices only in each instance – and periodically *Traction*, the official organ of the Australian Federated Union of Locomotive Enginemen, which he never reads. It is always to be found the day after delivery on top of three months' empty Snappy Tom tins and milk cartons in the bin, not even taken from its wrapper, as though the urgency of disposing of it has somehow the power to set in motion a whole chain of normally dormant procuratorial responsibilities.

By mid-September the false lucerne is flowering but there are no leaves yet on the oaks or the elms. One of the two most common local wattles, biveined hickory, is still in flower, but the most dominant odour in the cool evening air tonight, a strong, sickly-sweet odour not to every taste, is that of the native daphne, a species not native to Dog Rock, but one which has found the town so greatly to its liking it has come to dominate every ungrazed vacant block, every patch of virgin scrub, and all but the most carefully tended garden beds, whether of red basalt or black shale. Thriving best in the rainforest of the coastal escarpment, where it often attains a height of thirty-one feet, it flowers in September, producing in January a bountiful crop of small orange berries, each containing an abundance of sticky orange-red seeds, which when disseminated by the most numerous bird in Dog Rock, the pied currawong, have the capacity to colonize every local plant community, from the dry sclerophyll snappygum forest of the sandstone near the substation, where it seldom attains a height greater than twenty-nine feet, to the wet sclerophyll ribbon gum and turpentine forest of the gullies, where it usually attains a height of thirty feet six inches. Of the 776 local residents only five know the common name of this tree, which has killed in its time, through asthma or fracture of the neck, numerous local identities, and only one knows its botanical name: moreover, this scholar is not in the habit of speaking to his neighbours, whom he secretly regards as a job lot of ignorant colonials.

The earliest photograph of Dog Rock (known then as 'Calvary's Crossing') was taken in the year 1868 and shows the railway line – a single track as it was in those days – passing through a forest of peppermint, silvertop ash and rough-barked apple, most every tree of which has been ringbarked and a good many actually felled, so as to leave a morbid landscape bordered by dead trees and dotted with irregular stumps between two and six feet high. Digging out these stumps by hand is a chore the squatter puts off as long as possible, so that the fields, despite an appearance to suggest the recent passage through a sawmill of a large meteorite, are already fenced with post and rail and sown down to pasture.

Two houses, each in its way a precursor of things to come, can be seen in this early photograph: one, set amid stumps and standing roughly where Simeon FitzGibbon's greyhound kennel stands roughly today, is a shoddily erected stringy-bark slab hut built on the lines of a Gaelic blackhouse, but with an external chimney owing to the highly combustible nature of its bark roof; the other, within twenty-two yards of the railway line and later demolished to make way for the platform, is a cottage built to resemble a gatekeeper's lodge on a manor house in the Gloucestershire Cotswolds, but with a roof of galvanized iron to nullify the insulating properties of its walls of local sandstone.

This, unlike Cotswold limestone, cannot readily be split into roof shingles.

The contemporary equivalents of the descendents of these two archetypes house the present-day populace: if only the genius who invented the stump-jump plough had been born to bake bread on a fuel stove in a fibro blackhouse with an iron roof; and what contemporary Snowshill or Bourton could sneer at a village built wholly of petrified sand and roofed in cedar shingles, like some imposing simile of the coastline seen from a ship at sea?

Never mind: I observe Dog Rock as she is and not as she might have been, for nothing is more certain than that she might have been even worse than she is: a Barren Grounds, for instance, or a Cow Flat.

Under mysterious southern skies so full of strange and lavish constellations the names of which only Estivador Orloff, retired waterside worker of Buenavista Avenue has even known and he's forgotten, Irving Calvary, railway engineman, a cigarette dangling from his lower lip, gazes now over the tumbledown fence at the house of his next-door neighbour and cousin German Maurie Calvary, Renee's husband, a landless farmer, or fencing contractor, to give him the more usual title.

A fibro cottage the colour of a postman's shirt with garage to match, it stands on the corner of Tattersall and Tooth Streets with a roof of old red tiles in which the odd delinquent has been replaced by a white, yellow or blue surrogate. It is difficult to tell which side of the house is meant to be the front. Mail is addressed to Tooth Street, where the galvanized garbage bins are also to be found, but the letterbox, sitting askew a stringy-bark fence post and nine times out of ten falling off as I open it, is in Tattersall Street. Immemorial red brick foundations project six feet beyond two of the four fibro walls. A small ornamental plum, well cropped, is the only tree on a block divided by means of angle iron and cliplock fencing into several small paddocks. No grazing animals can be seen but a black tracker could infer, from the age and shape of the dried manure, an ancient stock horse and five merino wethers. Scattered about, often localized into patterns to suggest the construction of temporary shelters, are sheets of galvanized roofing iron, lengths of concrete pipe and

8

four-by-two, second-hand building materials such as windows, a rusted-out box trailer with a Holden spare, a quantity of uncleaned preused bricks, a mangle, several military duckboards, a builder's wheelbarrow well cemented, a billycart base in vinyl teak, three brand new BMX children's bikes with yellow knobbies, a plough disc fitted to three lengths of threaded pipe to form a barbecue, an unregistered Valiant Charger sedan, several large enamel bathtubs as used for watering stock, and a blue-painted children's combination swing and seesaw set of a make (Cyclone) very popular in Foggy Hollow. Numerous dogs, some running stealthily on chains, some roaming free, maintain a state of constant vigilance; red and blue heelers, pigdogs for the truck, a dainty toy poodle for the home. The chain of one rattles against a tub as others dispute the ownership of bones. Irving Calvary, without a thought in his bald head, is stubbing out his cigarette on the palm of his hand when he hears the engine of Dion Belvedere's approaching PE 250 Suzuki Enduro, ridden at speed, as it negotiates the sweeping left-hand bend by the railway bridge near the garbage tip two miles to the south-east.

I shall now stretch my powers of imagination to their fullest capacity.

Savouring the odd patch of mist in the hollows as a tribute to his considerable skills, a fearsome sight in Hawaiian shirt and black helmet with black visor, impervious to the cold, conscious only of a deep thirst for oblivion, the youthful Dion straightens up and throttles his mount to even greater efforts.

Who would care if he died this instant? He taunts Death by riding off the broken shoulder of the road – which some time next week, as a member of the Council pepper-and-salt gang it will be his duty to fill – onto the gravel at Christmas Creek corner, sending up a shower of ochre stones as his knobbies break loose and riding with the unmistakable verve and aplomb of one who has never come off. Indeed, since the age of three when he first learned to ride a two-wheeled vehicle, he has never yet dropped one.

He is not so much keen to get home at present as anxious to put as much ground as possible between himself and Lisa Goddard of Bonny Tops, who not twenty minutes ago on her parents' front porch – about the time I was setting rotten spuds to boil on my Kookaburra fuel stove for the cockerels' breakfast – confessed under questioning she still held feeling in her freckled breast for Bigfoot of Cow Flat.

Without either protest or condemnation Dion turned on his heel and left but he has since thought of a great deal he would like to say and he is going to say it tonight, over the public telephone, where no one will hear him. The problem is change for the phone at this hour, the pub being shut. But Dion Belvedere will find change, by God he will: he will find change if it means thinking harder than ever he thought before and if it means waking a total stranger he will lay his hands on a twenty-cent piece and he will tell the truth about Bigfoot, how he refused to slide his bike down the hill at Hell Hole, though Belvedere, at one point perilously close to The Drop (a fearsome abyss) had shown it could be done.

At the Round Table of Motorcyclists, Dion is the local Galahad; unwounded and fresh-faced amid the scarred, the halt and the corrupt. Let a rider once feel the sword of his enemy, Earth, upon his flesh and he never again rides with quite the same abandon. He may ride as fast or faster but at the cost of acquiring on his forehead the characteristic worry lines of one who has deliberately conquered his own memories and forgiven his own shortcomings. Drawn to vice, addicted to pain, he joins the great gang of those whom Death has claimed in Life; for Death withholds the Black Hand conditionally and those who fall just once are His forever.

The solitude and darkness of the open country road yield to the tamer lights of town. Dion's warhorse, the SD 900 Ducati Dharma with Contis, Marzochis and Pirelli phantoms, still under warranty, is having a bearing renewed.

Pensioners yawn and sip Ovaltine as heroes battle Forces of Darkness. At the far end of the vast Railway

Parade another hero, Balthazar Whitefriar, neglected postmodernist painter and poet, is taking his evening constitutional. As Dion Belvedere, filled with bitter resolve, guns down three gears to enter his own drive, he notes vaguely with some surprise a young man walking by the pencil pines; but as it is someone with whom he has not drunk, worked, gone to school or played sport, he takes no notice.

Newcomers enter Dog Rock and capture the town with comparative ease. Locals born and bred don't recognize them, don't know who they are, don't care to, don't know where they come from, don't know they exist. This is not the first time Dion Belvedere has noticed Balthazar Whitefriar, who has lived in Dog Rock now, on and off, five years, yet still he does not recognize him. Strangers are so alike; all strange. It is said of the local Aborigines (mercifully extinct) who came in great numbers to feed on the plump Bogong moth at this time of year in this place, that when they saw the White Man in His ship off the coast they ignored Him. When spears were hurled, it was too late. The invader was hidden in the fold of the eye.

Balthazar Whitefriar, who has never ridden a motorcycle of any kind, belongs to that timeless category of misfit and malcontent, the eldest son, who having been given every early advantage fails or refuses to make his way in the world and returns in his early to mid-twenties to live, figuratively under his parents' roof but more usually in a phoneless shed at the bottom of the garden, neither emptying the mailbox nor putting out the garbage, an irritation to his father and embarrassment to his mother, whose only consolation is that she is not the only one.

There are five Balthazars in Dog Rock, two of them locals and a source of utter bewilderment, two more, like Balthazar Whitefriar, unknown and unheard of. They are distinguished by artistic talent, an obsession with their plight, a sense of their own superiority, a reluctance to work, a gold earring in at least one earlobe and a fondness for soft drugs. Not one stands to gain the inheritance that might make possible the life he has chosen.

Balthazar Ganjadin is the son of a council worker's widow, Balthazar Prikpop a railway fettler's son. Balthazars Malbane and Dodgecastle live together in the old manager's cottage on Labour-in-Vain, the dairy long the subject of acrimony between Sambo Fargo, who denies it lies on the delivery beat, and the Postmaster, who insists it does. The bond between Balthazars Malbane and Dodgecastle is not, as some suppose, sexual; each holds the other in that compassionate disdain philosophers reserve for their rivals but no Balthazar is free to acknowledge the existence of any other and their intercourse – which goes on sometimes eighteen hours a day in the absence of the physical and astral travellers that call by at all hours of the day and night – consists of a keen psychological inquiry, stretching back to earliest childhood and leaving no stone unturned, and based on the unspoken premise on the part of each that the other is a complete fraud, hampered by an occasional suspicion that no two men could be more alike.

Balthazar Whitefriar, picking his way through the occult minefield that surrounds the Dog Rock (a Place of Power), cringes as Dion Belvedere mounts up and roars off again, this time clutching his sister's Darth Vader piggy bank in his clutch hand. He rides at a speed that given a suitable ramp would see him clear in comfort the mauve-painted ex-bank agency that looks straight up the main street. It is one of a tiny trio, none bigger than the third bedroom of a project home, which form, on Mondays from 10.30 to 11 a.m. and Fridays from 10 a.m. to 12.15 p.m., the mercantile centre of Dog Rock, where the sight of an approaching wife of a local businessman staggering under her sack of twenty-cent-piece rolls can precipitate a stampede of geriatrics hastening to cash their pension cheques. Note the large unshuttered window through which can be seen in the full beam of an approaching headlamp a cedar desk littered with expanding files and a mastaba of Gem Marg cardboard boxes filled with the town's taxation returns. A plate proclaims it the offices of Claude Caprol, semi-retired public accountant and holder of post office box 27 – which lies not 200 yards off, empty but for a glossy brochure I thrust in last thing Friday afternoon featuring matching wall units with a unique, wavy-edge design, among them an excellent storage unit at $83 – a septuagenarian in good health, whose white immaculate MGB sports car, long the envy of Big Owl and Farmer's Friend, who sit admiring it from their observation post on the park bench outside the African Mission Opportunity Shop, has never been driven at more than 40 mph, never in the wet and never on the dirt.

10.20 p.m. In the exchange the shutter for public telephone number 2 falls, activating a small buzzer which for the moment I ignore. I have pulled back the swivel seat and will shortly make up the camp bed on which I must spend the night. The pull switch to the fluorescent light will hang by my right ear and the log book, in which I will enter all calls, will abut upon my pillow next to the massive area code index.

I was hoping for a peaceful night's sleep and the sight of that shutter falling at this hour on a Sunday night causes me grave concern. I feel sure it will be some pimply-faced yobbo, who in the course of an argument with his girlfriend will either stay on the line for an hour and a half with frequent long silences or keep ringing back for the last word at intervals ranging from two minutes to thirty.

I allow the buzzer to buzz: sometimes they repent of having lifted the receiver. Like my father before me I am a sound sleeper and usually still in my pyjamas when the first telephonist arrives in the morning. Things get pretty busy round 7 a.m. and if you go back to sleep after the butcher calls the meatworks, as I tend to do, you don't have time to fold away your bed or change out of your pyjamas before the deluge.

My pyjamas have discreet, mother-of-pearl fly buttons but even so, the telephonists – decent, married girls – object, I understand, to coming on duty fresh and sweet-smelling to be confronted with a darkened room stinking of Champion Ruby, an unmade camp bed with rumpled blankets and sheets where the stools should be, and kneeling on top of it, in a frightful tangle and screaming at the subs, a tousle-headed middle-aged Pommy bachelor wearing a pair of blue-striped pyjamas.

The Postmaster has spoken to me about this matter, as he has spoken to Sambo about bringing the dog in, a bull terrier, but neither of us seems any longer capable of changing the habits of a lifetime. Sambo was most put out recently, when on one of his frequent car trips to the city – made for the express purpose of breaking the record for the greatest number of green traffic lights encountered on the Tewkesbury Road – the opening of a new section of freeway left him uncertain as to where to light the second of the two cigarettes traditionally apportioned to the journey.

At the moment I am taking down my trousers, a pair of blue acrylic postman's shorts. I wear shorts, winter and summer, as I hate the thought of something grabbing me round the knees. I suppose that comes from having played rugby as a boy. One of the few advantages of being a postman is an entitlement to free clothing, which does not, incidentally, include mittens or gloves, despite the severity of the Dog Rock winters. It is widely reckoned not possible to extract a letter from a mail bundle wearing gloves.

This can also be hard going with one's hands frozen stiff, but Sambo's hands after going very cold seem to become very warm, while I must bear the agony as best I can, and often return to the Post Office with my hands set in a claw-like conformation, the result of gripping motorcycle handlebars in a sleet storm.

Funnily enough, I don't seem to feel the cold in my knees at all.

Both Sambo and I have cupboards full of old uniforms and drawers full of shoes that date back, in his case, to the khaki shorts with the black serge coat, through grey, to current blue. We both believe in getting the full wear from an item of free clothing, and one of the great grievances of Dog Rock is that townfolk never know whom to blame for wet mail, as Fargo wears his uniform at all times, on duty and off.

The shutter of public telephone number 1 now falls as Belvedere switches cubicles. The cubicles are at the front of the Post Office within shouting distance of the exchange. In my underpants I shove in a jack and speak into the headset without donning it. The only other sub connected is 152, Renee's cousin Maureen, speaking to a friend in Alice Springs. This call was in progress when I came on and I know nothing of it.

'Number please?'

'Thought you musta been *asleep* in there D'Arce! Bonny Tops two three thanks cob.'

'The call will be twenty cents. Have you a twenty-cent piece?'

'Yeah, course I 'ave, y'drongo.'

'Do not insert your money or press the button until requested.'

I look round for the amber sheet of paper inscribed with the local area codes in pencil. I don't bother memorizing codes. Flicking the switch I dial Bonny Tops where another postman is making up a camp bed.

'Bonny Tops?'

'Yeah.'

'Two three thanks mate.'

A short hit on the button rings the subscriber's phone. Allow up to ten minutes for pensioners to hobble in from the yard. Don't keep ringing, you'll be old yourself one day.

'Bonny Tops two three? I have a call from a public telephone, please hold the line.'

'Insert twenty cents.'

Kaching.

'Press button A.'

Kaclunk.

'Go ahead please.'

'Look bub, it's me again: about what you was saying earlier . . .'

If we don't listen, do you blame us? The clock on the wall tells me it is 10.22 p.m. In eight minutes time the night alarm will cut in. I cannot bear the night alarm, it has ruined my nerves and destroyed my constitution, but I cannot turn it off without unlocking a glass door, the key to which is kept in a sealed envelope, initialled over the seal by the Postmaster and Head Telephonist both. When after 10.30 p.m. a sub lifts a receiver or an incoming call causes the little light to shine, a piercing electric bell rings out from a wooden housing above the shutters. It rings until I answer the call. Of course, if two incoming calls register simultaneously or if one comes in while I am processing another – I never did acquire the knack of handling more than one call at a time – then what sounds like a burglar alarm will be heard quite plainly over the phone. As a moment ago I was sound asleep I mustn't sound as though I know what I'm doing, and many an outsider has evidently wondered If I am not some sort of criminal engaged in robbing the exchange. I have actually put callers through to the police station and listened with surprise as they reported suspicious goings on at the Post Office!

On the night the fire broke out in the back of the Tipperary Reception Centre, a licensed restaurant cum caravan park visible to most of the town, I got myself in such a tangle the late alarm cut in for the first time in fifteen years. This late alarm is a huge black dust-covered klaxon housed in the roof that cuts in after ten minutes if the night alarm is still ringing. Both the Assistant Station-master, summoned on the independent signals network, and the Sergeant of Police, next door, woken by the late alarm, ran to the exchange door in their pyjamas and uniform (not respectively), but I could not hear them knocking, and would not have been able to leave the board, where shutters were falling like raindrops, if I had.

I am glad it was not thought necessary to install an alarm greater still than the late alarm to cut in after ten minutes should the late alarm go unanswered.

When eventually the Sergeant of Police fetched the Postmaster to unlock the door from the outside – the

ASM, having noticed the fire, had run round to the public telephone to ring the fire brigade – they found me, not, as anticipated, dead of a heart attack, but perched on the board in my bare feet, pushing up the shutters in a pose memorized from a postcard of a Balinese temple dancer.

When last the late alarm rang, another policeman, since posted west I believe, broke down the door to find Sambo, who was fifteen then, sleeping soundly.

That was before he began bringing the dog in, a bull terrier. The dog is there to rouse Sambo – which it does by shaking the legs of the camp bed to and fro in its strong jaws – but it will also attack an intruder, unnecessarily, in view of Sambo's physical strength: he can pack a private box so full of mail it cannot be cleared.

While waiting for the board to empty I make up my bed and assume my reading spectacles. I then take up my handbook to the youth hostels of England and Wales and my book called *The Cotswold Way,* which is neither a regimen nor a short cut to equinimity, but a long-distance footpath of 100 miles from Chipping Camden to Bath, countryside of which I am fond and which I visit every year of my life, with a stopover in Hong Kong on the way back never on the way out.

It is six years now since I stood among the ruins of Hailes Abbey and I will do so again in two weeks time when I take my annual October leave. As a bachelor I can well afford the air fare and my expenses, once I arrive in Britain, are minimal, consisting largely of B&B tariffs and the price of a ploughman's lunch. I have to visit Alick Sidebottom's elder sister in Bournemouth, as no one else does, and Murial Topwaite, who used to live in Dog Rock but now lives in a small granite house in Oban also called Dog Rock, I try to visit as well, and I always spend my first week in a hotel near the Elephant and Castle in London. As I have said on many occasions to people unlucky enough to find themselves sitting next to me in a bus, the minute I step off the plane at Heathrow and find I can open my eyes without squinting, I know I am home again and able to be my real self for a month, and occasionally a full six weeks when, as now, long-service leave has accrued.

I have walked all the British footpaths, from the Pennine Way where the vibram boots have worn a fissure in the peaks, to the South-West Peninsula Path across the muddy estuaries of Devon, and the Cotswold Way is like the others, difficult of access. Bookings at Bed and Breakfast houses must be made well in advance, and in Friday's mail I found an airmail letter addressed to myself – a postman who lives on his own beat breaks up mail quicker than one who does not – advising me there is no vacancy on the night of Tuesday October 16th in the Old Bakehouse at Stanway where the Way crosses the B4077. This is a blow, as the only alternative would seem the ten-mile hitch into Stow, where the town clock is in the main square, right on the wold and next to the hostel, causing me, when I hear it, to sit bolt upright waking the whole dormitory as I grope for the light cord that should be there and isn't. The last time I stayed at Stow I was interviewed by the hostel warden, a young New Zealander, having been observed shortly after midnight grappling with the straps of the six-foot backpack of the Californian in the upper bunk to my left.

If only those folk could have understood what I had for them in my *heart*. It's always a lavish greeting card in the underpaid, taxed envelope.

The best time to walk such a track is in April, before the nettles grow, but the weather in October is usually more certain and one often gets those clear, balmy days, of the kind Dog Rock enjoys at present, when a man can reconcile himself to exile in the ecstacy of what he has left behind him.

10.27 p.m. I draft in pencil a letter to the warden of the youth hostel at Stow-on-the-Wold.

10.28 p.m. I contemplate the portrait of the Queen of Australia, moved at my request from the post office broom cupboard and hung on the exchange wall. Both Sambo and I give careful consideration to the precise timing of our annual leave, the object being to saddle the

18

other with as much mail as possible, short of provoking violent retribution. When Sambo went off in April I found myself on the first Monday with the *Open Road*s, the *Reader's Digest*s, the *National Geographic*s and two lots of householders. He in his turn will cop the *Bowls* magazines, the electricity accounts, the RSL journals and the *National Farmer*. For the whole six weeks I am away (assuming I decide to return) Fargo will deliver and dispatch the mail by day and sleep in the exchange by night. His consolation will be overtime and the knowledge that if it is bad for him it is worse for me, who cannot sleep during my lunch hour as that is when the duck eggs, which could be anywhere, must be collected from under the Mexican pines.

10.29 p.m. A guilty thought of my eldest cat, not a well cat by any means, makes me frown as I monitor the lines to see if they're still busy. They are: I catch something about a cashmere sweater from Alice Springs and from the PT a sniff of tedium. My cats invariably die while I'm away, cooped up in that big stone house of mine like a TPO mail advice in an empty mailbag, and I carry over the British byways, heaped as it were on my shoulders, an invisible sack of ailing cats and household Leghorn cockerels imploring me to reconsider their well-being. In reparation I never leave them more than twenty-four hours at other times, and when recently obliged to travel to Hobart for a torsion bar for my Jowett Javelin, left on the Corkadah Mail at 3 a.m., caught a flight to Hobart from the airport at 9, made my purchase, caught a return flight, and was back in my own bed that same evening. For myself I'd have stayed for a game of golf, so say what the cat may, it cannot say of me I put myself first at all times.

Besides, there are things a man must do of which a cat understands nothing. If I had to choose between putting the cat down and never seeing Cheltenham again, I'd make the chooks' life hell for a couple of weeks, depend upon it.

That stroll down to Stanton from Laverston Hill through the green beech and trembling herb-robert has no antipodean counterpart for my money, despite the claims of the Dog Rock Tourist Information Office (Bernie's Bike Shop) to the contrary. In Dog Rock there is no twilight, no sense of departed majesty, no glory to look back upon; only a vague sense that the appropriate response to beautiful countryside, dotted with willow and etched in pine, is to stand looking as it with a sense of loss and one's hands firmly in one's pockets.

10.45 p.m. I fall asleep leaving the PT connected. On the punctate wall of the PT cubicle Dion Belvedere inscribes his initials, working with great precision and care. Dudley Semple the baker, who rode a BSA Goldstar in his youth, notable for an engine that got so hot it used to glow in the dark, and who went to bed tonight at 9.30 after making up a bag of dough with ice in the Thorbread Mixer, at last dozes off, his *Reader's Digest* slipping onto the bare boards of the bedroom floor. In the bakehouse the dough rises.

The moon comes up over the Dog Rock, a sandstone outcrop in the nearby National Park. Boobook, barn and barking owls enter the town on silent wings from surrounding bushland and sit, whitely, on the dead limbs of ribbon gums under the street lights watching for mice. An old dog foxtrots across the vacant paddock below the Wold Guest House, heading for Sikspak's hencoop. Grey kangaroos under the watchful eyes of exotic bulls graze the paddocks on the Cow Flat Road. Wombats, in relative safety for once, cross and recross the same thoroughfare. Dog Rock domestic bees, ever restless, process nectar in a handful of peeling weatherbeaten hives. Balthazar Whitefriar in the light of his grandfather's hurricane lamp rereads the poem he wrote last night, little realizing it expresses imprecisely what Dion Belvedere is trying to say.

Black-faced cuckoo shrikes, white-eared honeyeaters, boisterous red wattle birds – birds of the budding magnolia – nestle in uncomfortable newly built nests; the magpies are breeding. Seven-year-old Kylie Goodfellow of 27 Ninkum Street nurses a scab on her scalp tonight: her father Keith hurled rocks at the ugly creature responsible for twenty minutes. It sat unruffled in a telegraph pole. If Keith remembers, it's good conversation for the public bar Monday night and it goes:

'Someone oughta shoot those magpies, there's too many of'em. Currawongs too, noisy bludgers. Hear'em this mornin'? Gonna buy meself a bloody *slug* gun mate, tell ya straight. *Shoot* the bastards! Kid's not safe in the streets!'

Beware the indignation, but not good for the prospects of the Dog Rock cricket team Goodfellow couldn't hit the maggie; he fields in the covers. The cricket season begins in two weeks but there'll be no preseason practice for Dog Rock. A few of the schoolboys may get together for a warm-up but not the grown-ups; part of the challenge of the game, as played locally, is finding form without benefit of practice. It's all part of the old Australian sense of fair play. How unfair to those who don't practice – to those perhaps who *can't* practice (and who can say these don't exist on the far boundaries of the district?) – if others were to take an unfair advantage over them.

A man is allowed the full season to find form without risk of being dropped from the side but if by the semifinal (usually the last game of the year for Dog Rock as I can no longer be relied upon) the opposing batsmen are taking three runs every time he fields the ball – one for the chase, one for the stoop, one for the throw – and he's still deciding what stroke to play as the keeper tosses the ball to first slip, it is time for him to buy himself a Panama hat from a good menswear store and to accept with good grace that most painful of all sporting transitions, which some seek to pre-empt by taking up lawn bowls in their mid-twenties, and others defer indefinitely, scorning lawn bowls as a game for old men. The Barren Grounds third-grade team consists largely of allrounders in their mid-sixties.

But when all a man has to remind him of his youth, his footballing days being over, is his cricketing flannels till they go at the knees and his toe-capped boots, if he's been a fast bowler, good for mowing the lawn in, then his dash is done: he is over the hill like the town he inhabits, Dog Rock, which sees itself as growing and expanding where in fact it is shrinking and contracting.

11.45 p.m. Dog Rock sleeps. The Bowling and Recreation Club closed early. Those who overdid it last night and were pleading for glasses of Orchy this morning respect the moratorium with those who attended evensong tonight. Those 35 full-time students and those 75 children attending school, those 304 working people, those 337 people who don't work (including those 3 women with 6 children, those 9 with 7 and those 5 with 8 or more), those 57 children not yet of school age, those babes in arms, those Balthazars – Dog Rock, like decent towns the world over, respects the sanctity of Sunday night. It is an early night, a night for warm milk drinks, a heart-warming night, an undemanding night. A night for comfort and recuperation. A night for *Disneyland* and bedsox. Not a night to visit friends. No night to argue with the missus. A family night for those with families. If the boyfriend comes round, he must leave by 10 p.m.

Bums to mums come bedtime. Not a night for nookie but a night for staring at the wall when the light's out, not too long and not too hard. Life slipping away night. Dreadnight. Vague sense of all not well night. A muffled sense of something happening but too slowly to be perceived.

11.48 p.m. Despairing of hearing sense from *any* girl who works on the checkout at the Half Case, Dion Belvedere slams down the receiver and heads off home to grab some shuteye, waking in quick succession Ivor Cruikshank from Lancashire whose wife Nora cleans the school; Mignon Calvary who lives above the pharmacy with her Sydney Silkie and her memories; the dear sweet spinster sisters Iris and Boronia Lilywhite who have seen to the flowers in the Uniting Church, formerly the Methodist Church, sixty years; that odd pair in the pottery and half of Railway Parade. 'Disgraceful' is the verdict, and Trent Truelove, Inspector of Police retired, speaks of making a citizen's arrest.

22

Trains are louder but they're on rails and paradoxically soothing. Normally there's someone in the signal box, but because of penalty rates the station is unattended over weekends and the signals are locked in the clear position by means of closing lever 13, the key to which is kept in a locked glass cupboard on the signal box wall marked 'Dog Rock closing key' – meaning only one train at a time can enter the section Barren Grounds to Bonny Tops. At ten minutes to midnight the sob of a goods train is heard to the west, labouring up the long grade between Dolly's River and the Cow Flat Road. At midnight precisely it comes through Dog Rock, two 44-class diesel locos pulling a twenty-six-car stone train, local traffic, black hoppers laden with limestone from the King's Lynn Open Cut for the Bonny Tops limeworks. It can still be heard ebbing at ten past midnight. Two of the five Balthazars listen to it for longer still.

At the back of the shops there's an eerie blue glow competing with the white street lights. It's not a phantom or will-o-the-wisp, but Dudley Semple's 6,000 volt cyclic Simon Insect-o-Cutor, sitting atop a fridge filled with 1 kg Pinnacle yeast packs and cans of Schweppes lime. The bakehouse door is open because of the heat in the bakehouse. Three black and white bakery cats doze among the floursacks. The bakehouse blue heeler, expecting Dudley any moment, pads up and down the concrete walkway between the residence and the bakehouse, the nails of his toes broadcasting the fact he's a young dog, stupid as they come. The pleasant smell of alcohol has filled this low-ceilinged room, dominated on its eastern wall by a huge antique brick oven.

The days and months of Dudley's tenure, twenty-three years so far, tick over above the TV on the calendar from Evers & Co, suppliers of everything Dudley needs, from wafer crosses for his hot cross buns to red and green Cherrox for his cherry pies. The roofing iron of the vacant shop next door flaps and rustrattles in a wind that springs up and springing up in it is Dudley, wearing a white singlet, an off-white apron, schoolboy's shorts and schoolboy's shoes. He's yawning.

He turns the TV on full volume to the channel 9 late movie, reruns of the films of his youth nonstop midnight till dawn. They're all black and white so there was no point buying a colour television but the big antenna was necessary to get the city channel 9. Two hundred yards offshore a remote tropical island a curvaceous blonde is hauling a sodden, black-haired hero aboard a prototype speedboat while flunkeys dressed in the uniform of a private army sow furrows of the white wake with lead. The bakehouse roars as Dudley fires the diesel blower and opens the flues in the oven. Dr Scorpion rants and raves but we can't hear a word he's saying.

The plastic strips that prevent the dough crusting as the baker tosses and turns on his bed are removed from the roll of wholemeal dough, eight foot by three, on the laminated doughboard. First, the rolls: chunky handfulls are pulled off, kneaded, dipped in a white ice-cream container of sesame seeds, placed on a black tray glistening with pastry oil, slashed thrice with a baker's blade. Dr Scorpion's Chinese assistant laughs, pulls out a kris.

1 a.m. The oven is up to temperature, 700°. The diesel torch is turned off and the flues are rammed shut. We can hear Dr Scorpion now, he's most unhappy, nothing's going right for him. At 9 p.m. Dudley prefired the oven and opened the oven door to warm the bakehouse to prove the dough. The oven never gets cooler than 300° and won't be cold till Dudley is. Dudley uses a hundred gallons of diesel a week but he doesn't get a discount. You need to be a primary producer to get a discount on diesel in Dog Rock, and you need to have a degree in medicine or law to be able to buy a property.

The rolls are finished and proving on the trays between the TV and the oven. Dudley makes up to seventy dozen rolls Thursday night but tonight only fifteen dozen. Tipperary takes twenty dozen for the weekend if there's a wedding reception and local rumour has it the Wold Guest House is soon to change hands and become a rustic fitness farm. They should take a few wholemeal rolls and dampers once they get started.

Dudley could end up with a postman's wage, the way things are improving.

He pulls out the bread scales, weighted to 2 lb 4 oz, and breaks the rest of the wholemeal dough into loaves. The white dough that's been rising in the mixer bowl next to the fridge is carried to the doughboard like a bride. You'd never guess Dudley was over sixty years of age, looking at his torso. He's got the shoulders of a cabinetmaker.

1.15 a.m. What's Dr Scorpion up to now? He has the young lady in his clutches and he's rigged up a kind of trap in the jungle with her as bait. The chunks of bread dough, rarely so much as half an ounce out, are thrown in the divider, a little white flour scattered on the exit belt, the halves rolled, one in each hand, placed in the bread tins to rise. Any fancy rolls required? Dudley can't remember, so he heads off to the shop to check out the orders and in his absence the young man creeps through the jungle missing the trap completely.

Dudley fashions a few fancy buns, rolling the dough into strips with his palms, braiding the strips into knots. He rolls out three Vienna loaves. He doesn't need to watch what he's doing, but when it comes to the six strips for the poppy-seed loaf he concentrates intently, as no one makes a better poppy-seed loaf than Dudley.

And who else uses slowdough? Dudley put a mere 1 lb of yeast in that half bag of wholemeal flour: your fast-dough ghostloaf baker would have thrown in ten, not to mention gluten, molasses and artificial colouring. Slow-dough takes longer to prove but Dudley gets by on three hours' sleep and it tastes better and it doesn't mildew. Notice the way the ghostloaf mildews?

Why do people buy ghostloaves when they could be buying Dudley's bread? The bakers in the commercial bakeries have no control over the baking process. They never touch a lump of dough, all they do is flick switches. Their bread is always burnt or undercooked, hardly fit to feed to pigs. If you can call it bread which you can't.

1.30 a.m. Time for a smoke and a can of lime. The oven door is opened to speed the proving. Not much on order for Monday really. Why? Dudley could employ an apprentice and a pastry-cook if the town would only support him.

Why will the town not support Dudley?

That Dr Scorpion's a bit of a fool, does he really expect to outwit the young man? Looks the kind who would order a dozen ghostloaves a day, airfreight 'em in. Coloured wrappers. Bend them over your knee.

Mice won't even eat them.

2 a.m. The wind is blowing hard and the Dog Rock roosters are crowing in their first mass crow for the night. The dampers are rolled out and sat in white flour. The remaining white loaves are cut and divided, eight at a time. The halves are pummelled, rolled, thrown, occasionally hurled, into tins.

A good baker needs to be aggressive and that's why God, who loves His daily bread, has given Dudley Semple such a rotten life.

Each tin holds four loaves. The lids are kept in a wire cage on wheels in the middle of the bakehouse floor.

Dudley is sweating now, the sweat trickles off his biceps and shoulders soaking into his singlet. While his wife does the family wash later this morning Dudley will tend the shop, presenting free cupcakes to any child who walks in the door. Makes cupcakes late in the afternoon.

The oven is back to 500° and there's soot all over the bloody door. Burner's playing up. One tank loaf is rolled and put in the two-loaf tank tin.

2.13 a.m. Shutter number 63 falls in the exchange causing the night alarm to ring. I am swimming upwards from a deep cistern like the hero on the baker's television set. I am struggling to reach air, my lungs bursting. Above me I can see the sun, watery white and undulating. I am five years old and have just punched my sister, the honourable Mary, in the guts. She's crying so loudly Mother is bound to hear and she won't be able to have babies now. Shut up, honourable Mary.

Red-back spiders crawl through cracks in the skirting chickens escape through holes in the fence hot water runs to waste milk boils over on the fuel stove.

At last. My finger in the dyke wall. The heart is pounding.

'Numba please?'

No answer. The line is dead. An electrical fault has caused this shutter to fall and it's number 63 *again!* I write a *stern note* to the head telephonist, requiring that the techs go out I can't even think of the bloody sub. It happens too often, with 63.

As I snuggle up to go back to sleep it occurs to me the shutter will fall again.

Tape it up?

Too risky. Just my luck an escapee from the Prison Farm breaks down the door of sub 63 later that same evening.

Half a piece of tape perhaps?

Blast! Possessed by one of my proverbial furies I pound off to empty my bladder. I wanted the day in the garden! I *must* get my spuds in before I take my holidays!

Dudley Semple divides the remaining wholemeal dough and puts it in the bread tins. It'll probably wind up as breadcrumbs. The seven continental rolls are divided with a wooden baton and oiled to stop them sticking.

Resting in a roof-rack are three big peels fitted with thirty-foot handles. There's a hole in the window over the doughboard where a peelhandle went through a few years back. It's covered with brown paper for the time being. The oven is smoking a bit tonight so Dudley takes one of his flour-sack mittens from his flour-sack mitten dispenser (a skyhook), wraps it round a peelhead and swabs out the oven, switching on the oven light first. The oven light looks a bit like a bedlamp. The oven is deep and moist and warm. Tins, trays and dampers are stacked in the oven, thrust in stiffly on the peelhead. The poppy-seed loaf is sprinkled with water and poppy-seed.

3.19 a.m. Shutter number 63 falls in the exchange causing the night alarm to ring again.

The oven door is shut. The big steel tray on wheels is moved into position by the oven from under the loaf divider outlet. The wheeled tray, larger still, is moved to a spot near the fridge in the flour room to collect the loaves that have to be sliced in the Mono Universal Slicer.

The rolls are taken out of the oven and put back on the proving trays.

The bread is taken out of the oven and shaken from the bread tins onto the steel baking tray.

The dampers are removed from the oven. The bread and the dampers are wrapped.

4 a.m. It's a windy night and the roosters are crowing again.

4.30 a.m. A Volvo sedan leaves the pub car park in the dark, drawn towards Sydney.

4.37 a.m. Shutter number 63 falls in the exchange causing the night alarm to ring.

4.46 a.m. Bushy Tindle wearing a stockhat drives round town in his Valiant Charger collecting a fencing team which includes a reluctant Balthazar Ganjadin.

The bread can now be sliced and the orders made up.

At 5 a.m. it is still dark but the roosters are crowing. A few early workers gulp cups of coffee while idling car engines to wake the neighbours. Between 5 a.m. and 5.10 a.m. two cars pass the Post Office and a yellow ute passes the pub on the opposite side of the line. Neither the vehicles nor the men driving them – hard men, who breakfast in artificial light – are known to the town at large.

5.17 a.m. A down train goes through, slowing to pick up Irving Calvary in Akubra hat and grey cardigan with ancient Gladstone bag.

5.26 a.m. One of Dog Rock's three semitrailers, the Ford Louisville of Hiram Hamburger, heads off for the coal loader. He'll get in two trips today and pay off the rates.

5.30 a.m. Dawn breaks to the sound of dogs barking, cats fighting and bullocks bellowing. The roosters are silent. Cars of many car pools wind through Dog Rock making no sense in the direction they take, till one by one they head off for various oases of local employment;

the DMR road dumps, the Council yards, the factories of Bonny Tops. One at 5.35, one at 5.40, two at 5.45, one at 5.55; the Greta Garbos are late as usual.

5.32 a.m. Shutter number 63 etc.

5.35 a.m. Rick Cotter the Dog Rock milkman drives up to the shops in his battered Bedford one-tonner. He seizes the thirteen maroon plastic milk crates strewn outside the Zinnia cafe and takes them off to his minuscule depot next to the tractor factory. The shopping centre's sole remaining canvas awning, outside the pharmacy, flaps in the wind.

5.45. Kookaburras laugh and at 5.50 magpies and drakes join in. At 5.55 the currawongs start and the roosters join them.

A word on these Bertie Woosters: 61 Dog Rock residents keep laying hens in their backyard and one keeps laying hens in his front yard. Of these only 20 keep roosters but of those who keep roosters one keeps 7, one keeps 4 and one keeps 3.

Those who don't keep hens have worked out it's less trouble and no more expensive to buy dreggs at the Safeways. Of those who keep crossbred pullets only, most keep six – something there is that does not like to see five hens in a chicken coop – and either supplement what eggs they get with dreggs or do without omelettes and sponge cakes for up to three months at a time. Those large families who keep a dozen or more hens up to the legal limit of twenty and beyond, either find themselves with insufficient cackleberries for their own needs or, seasonally, with so many they don't know what to do with them. As the old practice of pickling eggs using the substance Eggpikla in conjunction with a Fowler's Vacola bottling outfit has disappeared from Dog Rock, if indeed it persists anywhere in the civilized world, these surplus eggs must be sold at a loss to neighbours or bartered for zucchinis, both practices proscribed by the Egg Board, which is not, as might be thought, a large piece of dead wood, but a State Government Authority set up to interlope between man and hen.

Keeping a rooster in the backyard is a vice for which there is no justification. Hens prefer life without a rooster, particularly if the rooster is a Light Sussex rooster, which in Dog Rock he usually is. The rooster will always have a favourite hen – recognizable by her battered appearance – on which he will bestow his favours more or less exclusively, so the vast majority of eggs will be infertile anyway. The rearing of chickens by the amateur is an uncertain business at best and at worst an utter waste of time and starter crumbles, with most of the miserable annual crop either frozen in cold snaps, suffocated by their surrogate mother, or taken by kookaburras and currawongs the minute they start moving about. When counterweighed against the nuisance of keeping heavy broody hens, which seldom lay but eat like horses, the cost of purchasing crossbred pullets at point of lay would seem most reasonable, particularly if the alternative is to buy a batch of unsexed chicks and hope for the best. It is not uncommon, having been consigned by rail a hundred day-old chicks, to end up three months later with thirty-seven crossbred cockerels scratching one another's throats out and not a hen among them.

Why then keep a rooster? Because if you're going to be woken by a rooster every morning it may as well be your own rooster.

Where hens can range free, a rooster is of use in keeping them together. But as Dog Rock grew, people came in who were neither farmers nor farmhands, just fanciers of poultry, not to eat but to handle and look upon with admiration. Such people have taken to the Privy Council their right to keep roosters in the backyard, from which it follows there exists in every country town a cell of ineradicable roosters.

What is remarkable is the way in which these roosters propagate their own kind.

Many a lucky man who owns a few acres on the outskirts of Dog Rock keeps himself a rooster, though his farmhouse be no more than twenty feet from his next door urban neighbour. The boundaries of Dog Rock are formed by roosters, crowing. Unfortunately, of the three

Dog Rock fowl fanciers only one is in this category: the others live within crowcall of the PO, and to be fair, the residence of Hector Pocock abuts upon a small gully, one of several such invaginations through which the town relieves itself of septic runoff. The PM himself suffers from Ancona: he keeps two roosters and a cockerel for Christmas, and within crowcall of his residence seven other householders have given up the struggle.

Hector Pocock is the Telecom tech who judges the Hardfeather at the Royal, and it is he who must repair shutter 63, this time properly let us hope. There are very few fowls Hector doesn't fancy, and those he's managed to appropriate he keeps in a complex of enclosed sheds in a backyard which terminates in the aforementioned gully, too steep for subdivision and so given over to Appaloosa geldings. The noise from his birds is minimal, as far as he himself is concerned, but residents on the opposite side of the gully such as myself, are obliged to keep roosters in sheer self defence. Hector keeps a minimum of seven roosters at all times, including a tiny and vociferous Silkie (for those who don't know, the breeding of this ludicrous feather-weight is the mark of the hardened fancier: the Silkie hen is a determined brooder and fanatical sitter on the nest, despite her size) which wakes Irving Calvary every morning at 5, and a lot of others who don't have to get up at that ungodly hour as well.

Hear him now, high-pitched and determined, proud to be so small and unique. The next rooster to crow will be Addiboy's Light Sussex. Now Gentle's big Rhode Island Red. Now Addiboy's Light Sussex again. Now the Silkie. Now Sikspak's Light Sussex on top of the ridge, and this is a critical call, for it throws down the gauntlet to the PM's pocket at the very beginning of the Cow Flat Road.

The PM's smaller Ancona crows. Now my own Light Sussex. Now Addiboy's Light Sussex again. Now Chuckyfried's Wyandotte.

Now the periphery comes to life, in the form of Balthazar Dodgecastle's crossbred mongrel; now the Light Sussex from Labour-in-Vain proper, and every rooster within Dog Rock and on the outskirts of Dog Rock is on his toes, thirty-one voices over two square miles, from Pocock's bantom Silkie to Pocock's massive and much beribboned Barnevelder.

One rooster alone is silent: the legendary feral Australorp of the Dog Rock gullies, oftener spoken of than seen, black as night, who lives among the lyre birds and moves in silence through the poultry yards of Dog Rock, accompanied by his friend Reynard the fox. What the one can't make off with the other seduces, and many and varied are his progeny.

At 6 a.m. the street lights go off and the wattle birds start up. A trail bike departs at 5.56 and cars at 5.58, 6.07, 6.12 and 6.15. At 6.03 two magpies alight to inspect the footpath outside the Zinnia cafe for potential breakfast. At 6.06 the milkman returns (driving on the footpath) with thirty-two one-litre cartons, four 600 ml cartons, four bottles and ten cartons of chocolate Moove for the Zinnia. At 6.10 a.m. two currawongs have a brawl on the steps of the Post Office: each is claiming Dion Belvedere's discarded Hubba Bubba. The milk truck moves along the street, disgorging seventy-six one-litre cartons at the greengrocer's mother-forgot shop and four one-litre cartons for Dudley Semple. Dudley himself is stacking local deliveries in his Holden panel van out back. The flier comes through at 6.20 a.m. all the way from Sapphire City, wherever that is. The cattle truck that went by at 5.55 returns with a solitary Friesian cow. At 6.27 the paper truck pulls up outside the newsagency and three large and two small bundles of papers and magazines are thrown on the footpath, rather than in the gutter where they belong.

6.30 a.m. Shutter number 9 falls in the exchange. The butcher is calling the meatworks and another vital day in the telecommunications of Dog Rock formally begins. I go back to sleep though I know I shouldn't.

The ladies are leaving for work in the factories. The newsagent arrived at 6.30 and has the billboards out by 6.40. Most people stop for a paper now, within choke distance of starting off. At 6.50 a second semitrailer,

Wallace Worrywart's UD, climbs the hill near the tractor factory. As many cars are coming as going, thanks to the car pool concept, though loners ride trailbikes. There goes Dion.

6.52. I'm woken suddenly by a mass of shutters falling. I'm in a bad mood, having had no sleep. Lots of people Monday morning want PPs in Sydney; a bloody lot of work for me.

6.52 a.m. The SM wanders over to the NA to buy a *Tele* before opening the signal box. As he ambles back across the street Dudley Semple drives past, still in his singlet, and hands him the tank loaf, duly wrapped, for a customer in Cow Flat.

6.55 a.m. Two unknown women in coats appear by the Zinnia, waiting for the Bonny Tops bus. They look subnormal.

6.58 a.m. The last of the town's three semitrailers, Ben Chuckyfried's M.A.N., heads off to Cow Flat to pick up a load of Shetland ponies and old English sheepdogs. Chris Calvry, no relation, sitting in the gutter waiting for a lift, waves ironically. The old Morris bus, driven by Jack Mouth in a grey dustcoat, picks up the two female passengers. The school cleaner starts on the boys' toilets.

6.59 a.m. The SM unlocks the signal box door and the door to the Dog Rock closing key. With this key he unlocks the Dog Rock closing lever and throws the blue lock lever and the red signals levers from position reverse to position normal. He then unlocks the down and up cutout switches. To all intents, the standard block system of traffic safe working is again operational. He then rings traffic control in Sydney for the day's timetable. Normally, this is phoned through at 5 a.m. but there was no one here at 5 a.m.

7 a.m. So much is happening now I can't begin to describe it. If I have managed to convey the fact it would not be worth describing I have achieved something; and yet I must ask you to believe, as I myself have been asked to believe, that among the inhabitants of this wholly decent and typical Aussie town, is a mass murderer so vile he could almost be a Welshman.

I am off duty in one hour and tired as I am I will tell you the story. Provided you don't mind standing in the wet garden while I dig my spud beds.

2 I don't know much about wombats and I don't know anyone who does. In appearance they're large, low, solid-looking beasts, dreadfully heavy on their sharp little claws and usually to be seen crossing the Cow Flat Road at night in a slow, unhurried fashion. Like rabbits they live in holes and do untold damage to fences. Despite this, no one interferes with them and not because they're protected by law: black snakes are protected by law but that doesn't stop us shooting their heads off. Their great burrows are often sited on hillsides to command a pleasant aspect and they've earnt a reputation for sagacity among the farmers whose fields they graze, because of their insistence on living alone, except in the breeding season. They are nothing like a badger. They resemble no other creature. A sturdy rugby league player locally as often earns the nickname 'Wombat' as 'Incredible Hulk' and I was once present at an interesting discussion among a group of long-distance hauliers in the public bar of the Dog Rock hotel, from which it emerged the wombat is the most feared marsupial on Australian roads. Given the choice of hitting head-on a wombat, kangaroo, echidna or wallaby – to be imagined as strung across the Nullarbor effectively blocking traffic – the hauliers agreed that having thrown their gearbox into neutral to prevent damage to the transmission while turning off the ignition to stop the fan going through the radiator, they would steer the bull-bar of their vehicle, assuming it had one, straight at the roo, especially in a car. Hit by a bull-bar a roo, like a pedestrian, is the right size to go straight up and over the top, which is not always true of the smaller wallaby; an echidna makes a nice job of your tyres; and the wombat is to be avoided to the point of rolling the vehicle down a bank.

So very inelastic and dense, a wombat is the right height to wedge itself under the bumper, and while a rolled vehicle can be driven on, with its front end done in it is often a write-off, as that is not a spare part always carried.

You can be sure then that when I saw that wombat I knew Fargo hadn't killed it with the Honda.

If we'd pursued the tank loaf earlier on this morning you and I, the one we last saw being handed by the baker to the SM (a day in the life of a tank loaf: I've watched less gripping sagas), chasing it by car the ten miles through the snappygum forest to Cow Flat, we might have seen, if we were lucky, a dead wombat by the side of the road. They don't seem to get far, and no matter what they do to a car there's never a mark on them, just the faintest trickle of blood caking their filthy snout. For the first few days they lie on their side as though resting. Then they swell up and their stout little legs stick out straighter and straighter as they turn turtle. Pobjoy, who's forty and has to push himself terribly hard to keep fit for hockey, tells me you can smell a dead wombie for miles when you're jogging through the forest. It's the duty of the pepper-and-salt gang to pick them up but if no one's looking they'll be kicked into a ditch where they can't be seen from the road. They can be smelt though and that wombat in the grass was starting to go off, even in August. Yet it couldn't have been there more than a day or Fargo would have hit it the day before.

I wish you could have seen him, it was all I could do to keep from laughing, though you can be sure I wasn't pleased at being pulled out of bed to finish the run, pension day and all. I'd had a bad night. Shutter 63 again. That was the first night it fell. Late last month, this was. Wednesday August 29th. Fargo had Cootamundra wattle pollen on the arms of his navy-blue sweater.

The bike was lying on its side some fifty yards from the Cow Flat Road, not the sort of place I'd take a bike to tell you the truth, but Fargo is an aggressive rider. You'd think he'd been injected with a gramophone needle if you got him on the subject of those five local letterboxes before which he is compelled to dismount. He speaks with admiration of the Canberra postman who took his motorcycle up to the fourteenth floor of an office block, using the lift. The way Fargo sees it, sidestands are there to be scraped on the road while cornering, and I wish I had a postage stamp for every scratch he's put in the rear-vision mirrors. Just for the record, the houses belonging to the boxes he can't reach in dignity are the architect's cottage in Little Gully's Road (down a flight of bodgy-built steps, this fellow); Pobjoy senior's residence in Railway Parade (on the transpontine side of a moat); the manager's cottage at Labour-in-Vain, or rather, Idle-a-While, as I believe it's called now since Arblaster dispersed the herd and sold it to Doctor Isbester (up a muddy bank, but worth a try in a dry spell); Mrs Topwaite's villa in Ninkum Street (surrounded by cultivars and defended by a row of sticks and a piece of rope as well: much acrimony over this, you may be certain, but the customer is right in the end); and most infuriatingly, Ghostloaf Grange, hobby stud of the bread magnate (eight feet off the ground on the back of a sculptured Brahmin bull and a full four feet from the fence: Fargo used to stand on the pedals here, but the bike invariably toppled over: he's a big lopsided man, is Fargo. I think it's that liver of his).

The householders, some of them blowing down the hill and you wouldn't catch me chasing after them, told the sad story: just past the snozzle where the water-tankers fill by a bank of false sarsaparilla are two little houses that get no mail. There are 82 holiday homes in Dog Rock, of a total of 365. I won't deliver householders to houses I know are empty but Fargo is not so fussy, and the more he offloads early in the beat the better for him later. He'd been taking his customary short cut through that three-foot-high wilderness of kangaroo grass to get to Arunta Close, a modern little street that houses the builder Amos Jennings, secretary of the Bonny Tops Water-Polo Association, when something caused him to come unstuck. When he saw me he got to his feet and started raving on about householders two days running and the kill-switch, which it pleased him no end having to use for the first time, but the effort proved too great and he sat back down by a tiny laburnum its growth stunted by horses' teeth, his head cradled in his brawny hands. I suspect he wasn't wearing his helmet when he came off but he had it on by then, which may be the reason he didn't answer when I asked what had caused the accident.

It's not the best view in Dog Rock from the corner of Cow Flat Road and Arunta Close, though it must have something to commend it or why would Brian O'Bastardbox, the eminent gum-tree painter, have bought Fiddlewood, that stately mansion on the corner there. Higher up the hill still, behind a hedge of Chinese hawthorn, is the halfway house for recuperating lunatics known locally as The Funny Farm, box 39: forty-seven pension cheques per fortnight.

Anyone for tennis? A bitumen court with net still in position remains from The Funny Farm's boarding house days when Dog Rock was a tourist Mecca. Banks of purple pigface, deodars and rhodos, hide to some extent a design bespeaking an unexpected Edwardian demand for accommodation and a frenzied attempt to meet it at all costs, in the form of tasteless fibro extensions to the sandstone core. The view to the west is of green rolling hills with stands of urn-fruited peppermint and here and there the glint of a new shed. It's no Vale of Eversham.

Will you look at this sorrel among these oats? I grow winter oats as green manure. I never should have let old Sikspak in with his cultivator, but I was in a hurry to get home that year as I'd had a nasty scare. Woke up one morning stiff as a board, couldn't move a bone. It passed, but you can imagine how I felt about the prospect of sitting twenty-four hours in a jumbo. My bladder's not strong you see, and I saw myself being offloaded in Bahrain by a steward using a fireman's carry.

I always see Doctor Opfinger when I get back from Hong Kong (you can't be too careful), so I mentioned it to him in passing. You know what he reckoned it was? Saturday Night Paralysis. Caused by going to sleep with your arm thrown over the back of a chair. Quite a different thing to Saturday Night Fever, apparently.

Sorrel's like peptic ulcer, when you get it you've got it for good. You can keep it under control but you can never get rid of it. Let it go to seed and God help you. Yet when I get back from Hong Kong I know I'll find it in flower. It doesn't just flower though, it sends out a host of horrible white creepers. Worse than a blessed raspberry plant. Almost as bad as a buttercup.

You won't believe this, but I had a passionfruit vine here once, oh yes. But if you're ever on your own, you'll find you don't go in for a lot of fancy foods. Spuds are all you really need, spuds and a bit of meat. I like a piece of pumpkin as well, but I've killed no tomcats this past twelve months, and pumpkins need tomcats. Unless they get a good early start, you're wasting your time with pumpkins here. They succumb to mildew well before the first frost and nothing gives them that good early start they need like a fat young tomcat. Don't worry about your compost, and save your horse manure for the spuds. Buy yourself a twenty-two. You'll be doing the birds a favour as well.

I couldn't waste time on Fargo when I saw that cattle dog. I can only assume Fargo hadn't seen it, it must have wormed its way through the long grass the way a sheepdog will. They were bred up from dingos, Dalmatians and sheepdogs by an Aboriginal firechief. I recognized it at once, it was only a pup, but I'd been on the point of complaining to Mrs Jennings that day it nipped me in the socks, that it ought to be put down, or failing that, kicked to death. People don't realize these cattle dogs they keep about the place as pets are half dingo. They're a working dog, and if they have no work to do they'll create work. I hate to see a lazy big cattle dog laying idle. Especially when he's laying idle at the side of the road and I'm riding by on a little Japanese motorbike.

No farmer in his right mind feeds them, you know: there's rabbits aplenty in the paddocks.

I say it's the fault of the regulations there aren't more prosecutions than there are. According to regulations, a dog's owner is liable to prosecution only if the postman's skin has been broken. Now you'd need one of those Tibetan mastiffs we're told run loose on the ashram (and that's one place will never get a telegram) to break your skin through half a pair of rubber gumboots, and in Fargo's case, half a pair of postman's pants. He didn't look to me as though he'd qualify. I could see bruises aplenty, especially about the left side of the face, but blood there was none. So I took the matter into my own hands.

Being a reasonable person, I assumed the dog had caused the accident. Maybe I was a little overtired, but I picked up a brickbat I found by the track and smashed it down on the pup's skull; death was practically instantaneous and I dare say perfectly painless as well. Then I did a brave and foolish thing; with the pup still in its death throes, I seized from its gnashing jaws the dozen or so pension cheques it was in the process of masticating. For this I received no thanks, I might add, from the PM or pensioners concerned.

That's not the phone I hear ringing is it?

Mind you don't slip on the lino as we walk up the hallway. When I bought this place it was owned by an old man who couldn't polish the floors because of his walking stick. I don't think they'd seen a coat of polish in twenty years. But I do love colonial stone houses.

'Hello?'

'Sergeant wants to speak with you, D'Arcy. Putting you through now.'

'Hello?'

'D'Arcy, you're a beekeeper aren't you?'

'Yes, and I've all the bees I want. Hold the line a minute, Sergeant, I think there's a key open. Carmel, pull your head in, will you?'

'It's not the line, D'Arcy. Both my upper and lower lips are swollen. I want you to get your protective gear on and come straight out to Miss Hathaway's house. You know Miss Hathaway's house?'

'I do indeed.'

'Bees are in the stables. Straight over D'Arce, quick as you like. By the way, I didn't see your name down for the State Pairs. Not playing cricket again are you D'Arce? Getting a bit long in the tooth aren't you D'Arce?'

The fear in which policemen hold the domestic bee is something I don't understand. This is my first swarm call for the year, and though I have tried to make it clear I don't consider it a favour to be asked to remove bees, I'm sure it won't be the last.

We'll go to the beeproof shed now where I do my extracting and store my stickies. You probably noticed those two triple-deckers under the old blood plum. A kero tin of honey is plenty for me. I don't want increase, and if they all decide to up and off, good luck to them. They're a nuisance but like peptic ulcers, once you've got them you're stuck with them. The main reason I keep bees is for pollinating the pumpkins.

Now where's my white boilersuit? Bees like white, it calms them down. Shouldn't need a veil, I like to let a swarm roll all over my bare arms, just to show people they don't hurt. Oh, they get cranky in wet weather if they're hanging out on a bare branch, but you can bet the scouts are hoping and praying to see a beekeeper when they get back.

The old straw skep, you don't see many of those today, do you. In bygone days, when people would have thought it a stroke of good luck to find a swarm in their stable – I'm speaking now of medieval England – they housed their swarms in skeps like this one. Of course, you couldn't stop them swarming and you couldn't get the honey out without killing the bees, which you did by hanging the skep over a piece of burning sulphur, but you had a sight less work and expense, though the honey must have tasted strongly. In those days, when every man kept a few colonies, there were so many bees about they weren't thought worth conserving. What a sight the hedges must have been in spring, full of swarming bees! You need to hive them well before the flow's on.

> *A swarm of bees in May is worth a load of hay*
> *A swarm of bees in June is worth a silver spoon*
> *A swarm of bees in July is worth not a fly.*

On that basis, a swarm of bees now would be worth a milking cow, but I won't be joining it to one of my colonies. It just might kill one of my quiet old queens, and I wouldn't like the worry of working a vicious stock with neighbours who hate me to either side. I'll just chase them up into this skep and shake them out in the bushes somewhere.

Boilersuit, skep, smoker, pine needles, matches, let's go: we'll take the Javelin.

Miss Hathaway's Hospice for Homeless Horses we're headed. If you ask me, the knackery is the right place for the homeless horse, and that's where most of them end up, after eating $4,000 worth of feed that could have gone to some useful purpose. You can drive from Cape York to Derby via Wilson's Promontory and all you'll see by the side of the road are horses. It's the same the Western world over; every little darling must have her own pony, and the commonest pedestrian on Dog Rock roads, evenings when the school bus is in from Bonny Tops, is a teenaged girl in her stretch jeans and checked shirt, clasping the bridle of her beloved.

Since the inquiry began – and when Fargo fell off the bike he began it – I'm seeing altogether too much of the Sergeant. Once a week we sit together in the Police Station and pore over the photo that was given us by the man in the black tracksuit. He gave it to us to keep the appearance of the implement fresh in our minds. We call it 'the implement' though strictly speaking none of us know what it is. We call it 'the implement' and not 'the murder weapon' for fear someone may be listening.

It's a terrible town for gossip, this. I heard that the day I arrived from any number of different people.

Cadwalloper's all right I suppose, if you like policemen, but I don't. It's not because I've broken the law, I just don't like their big flat feet. I don't like their dark blue uniform. I suppose that comes from keeping bees. Bees don't like blue boilersuits. I once saw a policeman

41

in a white boilersuit, a member of the police rescue squad he was, come here to rescue Bobby Calvary who'd trapped himself on a park ledge teaching himself to abseil – the only thing he'd ever tried to teach himself, the town was most disappointed – and I remember thinking to myself, *there* is a policeman whose company I might enjoy.

To his credit Cadwalloper doesn't drink and he won't take the turkeys pressed on him by the publican, but when I see him in Church I have the feeling he's there to see if the organist plays the psalms correctly. She learned on one of those little veneer organs where all you have to do is press coloured buttons. 'When the Saints' was the first tune she learned, I often heard her playing that. To her credit she wouldn't stop playing till I was a long way off up the street.

They hide when they see me coming, you know. I've seen them do it. I deliver mail to streets you'd think were completely deserted, if you weren't clued in to the telltale tremor of the curtains, the shadow on the fly-screen gauze – and if you want to be a real bastard, stop at a box for which you've nothing and pretend to put letters in – yet when I look behind me I see in the middle distance a whole host of little figures moving over the driveways.

There's only one person on the beat stands by a box waiting for mail. God, how my heart goes out to her in her nakedness.

As you're not pressed for time, I tell you what we'll do; instead of driving straight to Miss Hathaway's, we'll turn left and cross the railway bridge up past the pub to the corner of the Old Cow Flat Road. You don't get the famous vista of the sandstone chasms in the park from there, but who does, apart from the Wold Guest House and those twenty or so retired bank-johnnies who sit along the southern ridge on Broken Dream Boulevarde. To my mind, it's a far more typical view.

Look at old Dirk, he won't wave to me. Turns his back when he sees me coming. Others complain of the same thing.

Here we are then. A pleasant prospect of a dying town. I admire the construction of Cotswold villages, truth to tell I was born near one, but they have one modern disadvantage: they're dead. They are occupied entirely by city folk who went there to enjoy a village atmosphere, and in doing so, drove out the villagers by raising prices till there was no village left. Dutchmen and Londoners own them now, and peer through the roses at each other with a sense of outrage and disappointment. The same process is under way here. We even have our first subdivision, 'Panorama Estate', courtesy of Mr Casimir Hrubucek. It adjoins Miss Hathaway's hospice, fifty serviced one-acre blocks. He's sold seven, which amazes me, considering the price he's asking.

If we look south from this park bench – one of several placed about town by the Community Development Association for the benefit of breathless pensioners – we can see, I think, most of Foggy Hollow. We can see the white-painted boots on FitzGibbon's verandah rail, filled with dead geraniums. Over behind Badminton's horses (skewbald riding hacks and palamino geldings) is Calvary Street, which runs parallel to Railway Parade on the other side of the line. Those roofs are the roofs of the shops. Prunus obscures the signal box and the corner of the memorial hall from here. Do you like Bushell's tea? That is the back of the old butchery. There was no fridge in those days. The killers arrived by rail. The old yards used to stand opposite the Hobbit's shop. Jack Calvary, with Terry Derry one of the two best hockey players this town ever produced, took them out to the holding paddock where the Calvarys had their slaughterhouse. If we walked to the top of this knoll we could see it. The old Commer one-tonner is rusting away in the peppermints there. It had a canopy and took four bodies at a time. Quartered, of course, but even the quarters weigh up to 200 lb. You'd wonder how a little fellow like Jack could lift them into the safe. In those days, the first thing a butcher did in the morning was sharpen the teeth on his crosscut saw. He had to cut wood to fire the coppers to boil down the fat and the bones. The sugar company bought the bones and the tallow went by rail to the soapworks.

The pines you see on the skyline are the pines between the Wold Guest House and Buenavista Avenue. The local brickies are building speculative houses, a bad sign that. Look at the great big mausoleum Michael Mucklethwart built himself. Now what would a twenty-five-year-old bachelor want with a place like that, for all his being one of the most cultured men you'd ever wish to meet. I've never known such a man for music and drama. He lays bricks to the sound of music and watches five hours of tele a night. And look at the bricks he's used: I wouldn't think they fell off the back of a truck, there wouldn't be one of them left unbroken. Fancy face bricks, full of holes. Shatter easily, hard to work. Can't use a hammer and bolster on them, have to hire the diamond-tipped saw from Scotties at $80 a day. He's taking a day like this off too, he must be rolling in it. Through his garage window I can make out the Lightburn electric mudmixer and the forty-four on the back of his ute.

I can see old Sikspak's place on the ridge over the roof of the pottery shop. They've patched up the pottery roof, but to my mind the whole thing needs rebuilding. Rafters like a dog's hind leg. I guarantee most of those roofing nails are hanging in thin air. I can see Iris Lilywhite's lovely mauve seralia, but what a nuisance when it drops its dead flowers. And Balthazar's treehouse in the ribbon gum: I don't think he's been in it once since he built it, and it ruined Sikspak's skyline.

But it's not just what you can see, it's what you can hear as well. If I've a cert or a reg or a telegram, I switch off the engine. I take off my helmet.

I can hear the kids in the playground, it must be 11 a.m. I can hear the bush flies and the currawongs. I can hear a builder somewhere to the west, banging noggins in. Pine, I'd guess, and they ought to be oregon. I can hear Prikpop's rooster. I can hear the breeze in the willows on Newcomer's vacant block. I can hear the yapping of Renee's poodle pup. I think I can hear Miss Hathaway's gander. I hear a car climbing the hill near the tractor factory, a Japanese car. I can hear the trill of an eastern spinebill in Ganjadin's red grevillea. I can hear a loco near the Cow Flat quarry. Someone's thongs are flapping on the tarmac, a transient from the caravan park. No one here wears thongs in September.

I suppose we'd better go. Don't be fooled by the beautiful weather, much of the time you can't see a mile in front of your face in this town. Dog Rock is renowned for mist. Right overhead, the coastal and the continental weather patterns confront each other. The clouds go several ways at once. As we are also that place where the city meets the bush, we can boast a host of different bird species. The Indian mynahs from the city appeared within a week of the Balthazars. Both came up the freeway.

The five to ten acres Miss Hathaway owns – pardon me, but I can never bring myself to describe a parcel of land as a 'ha' – what a thing to call a parcel of land, a 'ha' – is part of the old Arblaster estate, which once stretched all the way from Cow Flat to Plymouth, from the railway line to the park. Labour-in-Vain, or rather, Idle-a-While, is all that's left of it, and Arblaster recently sold most of that. Miss Hathaway is of the short-haired spinster breed, and spends a good deal of her time walking to and from the rectory. She bought the place from Cedric Ruse, who built the stables without a permit, as you can see from the fact they have no gutterings; the brickwork is starting to crack at the back and the awning has warped.

Here he comes. Oh God, he's collected a couple of stings, we'll hear it now. The way his eyes are closing, I'd say he tried to pull the barbs out. You must never do that: squeezes all the venom from the venom sac. Far better to brush them off with your thumbnail.

'Jesus, D'Arcy, you've no idea of the trouble you're in fella. This poor old sheila's been ringin and ringin and . . .'

'What are you on about, Sergeant? And why did you

have to interfere with the bees? I suppose I'm expected to settle them down.'

'If you can settle these blighters, I take back everything I ever said against you. Now there's one horse still alive in there, and we want you to go in and lead him out. For God's sake, go steady, D'Arcy. It's old Bottler, the oldest horse in the southern hemisphere. If he kicks you he might break a leg.'

'I'm sorry, Sergeant, there seems to be a misunderstanding. I brought this little skep along, thinking I was here to hive a swarm.'

'You mean, all hanging together? There was never any question of that. You're lucky Miss Hathaway had the sense not to leave her house when she heard the stampede.'

'And what time was this?'

'Just after seven o'clock this morning.'

'And what's the woman's phone number?'

'Sixty-three. You should know that!'

I think I'd better take a look. I never knew a swarm to leave a hive at dawn. Foragers work till dark but they don't leave home at dawn. One of the reasons you point your hive east is to tempt the scouts out early. Those bees must have been in the stables overnight and one of the horses took to them at first light. I've never laid into a swarm with a flywhisk and a pair of false teeth, but I guess they wouldn't like it.

Ah yes, I can see them now.

I tell you what, we might go home and get that veil of mine.

What a beautiful morning! The air is thick with the scent of native daphne. The jonquils flowered, as they usually do, in autumn. They can't make head nor tail of the seasons here.

The reason a beekeeper wears a veil is not because he's afraid of bees. One of two things happens when you get stung a lot, as you do in your first season: either you become immune to the stings or you get very, very sensitive to them. I've known beekeepers sneeze, wheeze, go into shock, even die from a single beesting. These are men, in my opinion, who should be debarred from eating honey. I stopped swelling up after fifty or so, but it depends on your attitude. If you're determined to endure what they can inflict, if they can sense you relish the conflict, they will reconcile themselves to being robbed, though they'll never actually enjoy it. They were on earth before mankind and they will be here when mankind is gone. Once you come to an understanding with them, you won't be stung nearly so often, and the stings you do get won't worry you, unless you get them in the eyes, up the nose or on the pharynx. If you get stung in the eyes, up the nose or on the pharynx, you tend to lose the quiet composure so essential when you're working bees, and you might even end up dropping a frame of bees, or perhaps a super. So you don't wear gloves, but you wear a veil.

Mind you, because his eyes are swelling up doesn't mean the Sergeant was stung on the face. He was most probably stung on the head, in the part of his stringy blond hair. Bees get very easily tangled in hair, which is why you should always wear a cap when you're handling them. I once collected 300 stings in the space of two and a half capless minutes. I was on my way to Church one humid morning, when I thought to myself, is that lid skew-whiff? It was the quietest colony of bees I'd ever kept. They must have been opening a queen cell. There's always that rare occasion on which a colony doesn't want to be interfered with. They were most apologetic about it a few days later, I might add.

It's said a thousand stings can kill a man, so if they've killed five horses this morning they've lost a few workers. Usually, bees don't sting like that away from their hive, it's got me puzzled really. More the sort of thing you'd expect from African bees, and those were golden dagoes.

Right. Now you see I've taken the precaution of putting on a balaclava under my cap, a thick, turtle-necked Fair-Isle sweater under my boilersuit and leggings under my rubber gumboots. Despite this, I fully expect to get stung. A man can dress himself to the point he can scarcely fit behind the wheel of a vehicle, yet a vicious stock will find a way of communicating its point of view. As vicious stocks are the hardest workers – and what makes them vicious is the sight of all those useless bloody horses doing nothing all day – the full-time bee man often keeps bees of a temperament the amateur would not wish to know about. I had the rector explain it to me once, by a process he called 'tunnelling'. When 30,000 angry worker bees attack the bee man in his boilersuit, some are able, by sheer dint of numbers, to penetrate the boilersuit, using the process that has given us Pacman and the transistor radio. They don't have to go through the boilersuit, or between the buttons, or down the neck or up the sleeves. As I understand it, they dematerialize, but speaking broadly, where there's a will there's a way, and there's no will in the animal kingdom compared with that of a savage stock of bees, their brood exposed to thunderstorm.

That's not thunder I hear, is it? Thank God. Just a semi with a load of roofing iron hitting that hump near the PO where the water main burst after Col Cannon swore blind it didn't need tapping. I can see roofing iron's back in fashion, but it's no good round here. Too wet a district entirely. Rusts out in no time. Look at this roof of mine, now I've so many ice-cream containers round my house to catch drips, you'd think I was watering 30,000 cats and not the three I do. If I could I'd get rid of those, but when you've got chickens and ducks you've got rats.

Get in the car, I'm trying to think whether shutter 63 was down when I went off. Quite likely it was. If I'd seen it fall from the corner of an eye while busy I might not have bothered with it. The night alarm cuts out at 7 a.m. and I might not have bothered with it after that. I'm glad now all my complaints are documented. It is a fact Hector can find nothing wrong with the line and it never seems to play up when Sambo's on.

Here we are again. I'll head off for the stables and you best stay in the car. If you see me coming back at a bit of a jog, make sure the windows are wound up.

•

Time for lunch. The bees are gone. Up and off while we were away, and Cadwalloper didn't even notice they'd gone, let alone note the direction they flew in. Did you hear her abusing me? It's a wonder. I could hear her through the veil and balaclava, I suppose I owe that to being a postie, I'm used to listening to complaints through a helmet over an idling engine. Not my fault your phone was out of order, I said. Out of order, says she, we had the line tested while you were away and there's nothing *wrong* with this phone! That's as maybe, said I.

She straight out accused me of causing the death of those horses. Cadwalloper stood by and said never a word, I tell you I find that hard to condone. Tired as I was I came when he called, and all I got for my pains was abuse. I told them straight, I said you needn't bother calling me next time.

Now the reason we're heading towards Cow Flat is I want to show you the site of Fargo's accident. You will understand this whole business better if you see where it all began.

The more I think about those bees, the stranger the whole thing seems to me. Something about it doesn't quite click, if you know what I mean. Did you ever see such dreadful stables, by the way? Did you hear the roof flapping in the mildest breeze? Bolts on the doors not plumb with the boltholes, grit and millet from Ruse's canaries still in evidence five years on, draughty and damp – yes, I know I'm still wearing my veil, but thank you for drawing it to my attention. I can drive safely, I can see quite well through the holes. Beekeepers often drive with their veil on, specially when they're moving bees. Never try to hitch a lift from a man wearing a bee veil.

Well, the queen must have survived. They wouldn't have gone far without her. That's if she was there to begin with.

I suppose you wonder what I mean by that. Well you see, when Miss Hathaway accused me of killing the horses, I thought she was meaning by means of the bees, and I must confess I felt a certain pang of remorse at not having thought of that myself. She meant the phone, but I followed it through in my head, nonetheless. Cadwalloper assured us he had carefully checked in the vicinity of the stables for vehicle tracks and found none – just the sort of thing he would do, I don't blame you for wanting to speak with me and not him – yet from the way they were flying about, as you saw, I would say they were not a swarm at all. I would say they were familiar with the lie of the land. I would say they were in their own territory. Which means they were no more than two miles from home. And I'm the only bee man hereabouts, if you ignore, as well you might, Ursula Topwaite, and the legendary Terry Derry, who hasn't been seen since World War II.

I'll check my own bees while I've got the gear on. They need a full spring check anyway.

The wombat was here, right here, in this long grass. Evidently struck by a car, it must have crawled over here to die. Fargo would have hit it flat strap. Pension cheques were strewn everywhere. It's hard for a member of the work force to appreciate the nature of this catastrophe.

The very fact the mail was going to be late on pension day was catastrophic enough. The bike was cactused. The mail would have to be delivered by car or Bernie's penny farthing. There are 285 pensioners in Dog Rock of a population of 776. A good many would already be on the phone to the PM, wondering why the postie was late. The pension, you must realize, is less than generous, and many pensioners would be skint, unable to buy their fortnightly baccy till the cheque was cashed. The tension in a PO on pension mornings, when the mail's being set up, is unbearable. Normally, should I find in the mail, say, one of Sharon Cannon's Medicare refund cheques, on which the address is always given, through computer error, as 'Red Bums' not 'Red Gums', I take it round to the counter to share the joke with the PM and any customers present. Not pension morning: pension morning Fargo and I set up and get out as fast as we can, to avoid those endless phonecalls that begin, 'Mrs Orloff of Buenavista Avenue has asked if I can please pick up her pension cheque in person this morning. She has to catch the bus to Bonny Tops you see, and she was wondering . . . '

A postman is fully within his rights to reply 'The mail will be delivered' and hang up. But we try to do the right thing by the customers, even those 773 who leave us nothing Christmas Eve.

It was while I was picking up the pension cheques I first set eyes on the implement. A lot of other mail was scattered about as well, some big stuff, parcels and the like – 'OAs' we postal workers call such things, which stands for 'Other Articles' – and shockingly enough, that wretched pup had chewed the address off a good few of them. There was a record of the Alban Berg opera *Votsit* from the World Record Club for Ivor Cruikshank, the sort of thing I put behind the screen door and Fargo frisbees into the flowerpots – Ivor refused delivery on this, said it was so badly damaged he just couldn't listen to it; a pair of plastic pilchers and a porcelain paperweight in a padded postal bookbag for Bryony Belvedere, who recently had another baby at the age of forty-five – she was in the Post Office complaining about it the other day, and the PM says, you could have said no – torn to pieces; some *Reader's Digest* condensed books, you can almost taste the sugar, but in those big heavy cardboard containers you could safely drop them over the fence of an ashram. Not a box on the beat will fit one in; a parcel of *Watchtower*s for the Latvian and I think some *Hansard* for the secretary of the local branch of the National Party, which goes to Ben Chuckyfried as we don't have one – someone told me once he voted National so I thought I'd try him. He never brings them back. There was Sidebottom's *Muswellbrook Chronicle*; Dulce Dwyer's *Arthritis and Rheumatism Council Newsletter*; the rather raucous and aggrieved *Voice of the Ironworker* – I bundle these but Fargo OA's them, why I'll never know; the *Shorty Ranger Fanclub Newsletter* for Rayleen Addiboy; a

Rydges for old Dirk D'Oilycart, which should have been delivered back at the garage but got left behind in the general stress of pension morning – the sort of journal I don't like, you could slip it from its wrapper and read it in a quiet moment, if you weren't strong-minded (you never saw a postman buy a *Newsweek*, now did you); *In Britain*, for Mrs Topwaite (can't open that; plastic-sealed like a piece of pornography); *Pointer View*, the organ of the German Shorthaired Pointer Society – it's no wonder I know who gets what, even without an address. How many German shorthaired pointers do you think we need in a place this size?

There were two parcels though that had me beat. Neither had an address and I couldn't decide what they could be just from the mere look of them. One had a piece of string attached and the other, very heavy and to the right of the bike, was in a sort of shell casing. I opened the one with the string attached first. Strictly speaking a postman should never open mail and I never have, though I read the postcards, all postmen do. Think twice before you write your holiday lies and exaggerations on a postcard.

I opened it in front of the PM, with the PM's full approval. It contained a 9 ct gold bangle, a Rabbitoh cloth badge, a pinafore from the Land of Let's Pretend, a seamaster torch and a pair of puce pantyhose. I saw at once it was meant for the Nightingales, but the other one had me stumped.

Imagine if you can something between a Swiss army knife and a plumber's eel, with elements of modern sculpture, articulating at five points along the midline, with a pipe reamer and a bass-drum pedal at one end and a corkscrew fitted to a camshaft at the other, precision engineered. We were astounded. The more so when Tom Bala, who trades as the Hobbit, said it wasn't his.

Fargo had amnesia. For seven days the implement was kept in the poste restante. The PM showed it, tongue in cheek, to everyone who came into the place. By the time it left for the DLO the town was sorry to see it go. Council workers were good at suggesting uses for it, and thinking up reasons why their best mate hadn't come forward to claim delivery. They weren't even close, as it turned out.

The man in the black tracksuit and Dennis Lillee moustache appeared in the company of the Sergeant one afternoon, and asked to speak to the PM and me, in private, if this were possible. As it wasn't – I was stacking coin from the PT for the PM to roll – we went to the police station at 5 p.m. that evening.

'My name is Detective Sergeant Wayne Something Or Other,' he said. 'Some little time ago this item' – he produced it – 'was sent by you to the Dead Letter Office, where in the course of routine examination, it was thought to have contravened postal regulations. Accordingly, a uniformed police officer was called in.'

He paused for emphasis, holding the implement at arm's length and giving us each the hard eye. If we were concealing anything, he would sense it. Satisfied as to our ignorance, he went on:

'Have you postal workers heard of the Queen's Park Ripper?'

Lives there a man, woman or child over the age of five in this nation who has not? Mind you, I find no mention of the Ripper in the *Guardian Weekly*, to which I subscribe.

'I take it you have heard of him. I say "him" not because of sexism, which far be it from me, but because no woman, not even an East German, would be capable of the sheer brute physical strength the Ripper has shown on occasion.'

He produced a photo. It was the photo of a woman's body, lying at the foot of an escalator. The PM took one look at it then rose from his chair, moving unsteadily towards the door of the residence. Cadwalloper steered him at the lockup and pushed him into the right-hand cell.

The woman's corpse was not a pretty sight but then, she was not a pretty woman. From the mean frequency of the bumpers on the platform, I could estimate the time of day as early morning. Was this then the woman the papers had described as 'a raving north coast beauty'?

'So this is the Ripper's second victim.'

'You've been following the case closely postie.'

'I can see the board bumps on her knees.'

The PM returned from the lockup.

'The Ripper was disturbed on his last rip, boys. Within a block of his last victim's body was found an instrument identical to this.'

'Whew,' said the PM, drinking in the implications.

'Come on you guys, what *is* this thing? So far Scientific Branch hasn't come up with a solitary lead.'

I wondered to myself if Wayne drank Cinzano. I could see his tracksuit had never been washed. No telltale specks of tissue paper.

'Postie, I want you to keep your eyes open. If you see another parcel about the right size, hold it and alert the PM.'

'Excuse me,' said the PM. 'Are you implying the Ripper is a Dog Rock resident?'

'Not necessarily,' said Cadwalloper.

'I'll have to take this thing away but I'll leave you guys a photo. If you find another implement, contact me immediately. And keep this whole thing to yourselves, okay?'

'Could I please be supplied with a list of the Ripper's victims.'

The Sergeant smiles at the plainclothes man.

'We don't want you solving the mystery, D'Arcy. You stick to delivering the mail.'

'Excuse me, but you asked for my cooperation.'

'We don't want you opening the mail. We don't want you listening over the phone.'

'I beg your pardon, I never have and I never would!'

'Then what can you hope to learn?'

'I'll arrange for the postie to be sent a copy of last month's *Bulletin* magazine. We use it ourselves. Care of the PO, right postie?'

'I have my mail delivered to my home address. Even the heavy parcels.'

'For God's sake, D'Oliveres! Care of the PO will do nicely.'

.

I'd read it of course, in fact, I'm a subscriber. I commence investigations tomorrow with a phone call to Miss Boysen of Bindara Bee Supplies. Provided I get a decent night's sleep, and you know, I have the feeling I will.

3 Now who among us would have reason to kill sufficient to make a trip to the city? Practising farmers have private boxes. Retired farmers, who often move to town to be closer to the Bowling Club, dislike city values, but have no knowledge of the city beyond the international air terminal, the wharves, the outer stand of the cricket ground, the showground cattle pavilion and the shopping corridor bordered by the local equivalents of Marks and Sparks. They could hardly be expected to Rip their way through the back streets of the inner city. Our yobbos, who very likely could, as they travel as far afield as Broome for hamburgers, are well disposed towards city values, prostitution and topless bathing in particular. They might heckle but not, I think, disembowel, though I could be wrong here.

I hate to agree with the Sergeant, but a recent arrival does seem the most likely suspect. A foreigner, I should imagine, we have a host of foreigners in Dog Rock. You should see the overseas mail we get Tuesdays, aerograms mostly, from friends and relatives abroad, but a fair few postcards from travellers in transit too: nuns visiting the Holy Land, children begging their fare home from Asia, parents and business associates wishing we could all convene in Venice: thank God I was never in Venice. The only place more popular than Venice with a touring Aussie is the beach at Bali.

Trafalgar Tours take them to see the Best of Britain in twelve days, you know.

I've never thought of London as foreign and I'm pleased to see Aussies don't either. It's as much home to them as it is to me. Take Arblaster, who's been to Britain twice in the past four months; he says he's never enjoyed television so much since he's been back. He came back on August 28. There's nothing like being able to say to the missus 'We've been there'. He had to return because he missed seeing the heather in flower the first time.

That photo of Myfynwy Milligan, the Ripper's second victim: twenty years old, on the pill, a queen of the drop at Byron Bay, she was working when killed as haruspex at the Hartebeest, a high-class brothel. Her job was to read the entrails of sacrificial animals and interpret auras, phases of the moon and the pattern a bottle of Dubonnet makes when broken over a brass fascinum. She stayed overnight at the Dog Rock youth hostel once in the course of a cycling tour, and was thought to be saving for a trip abroad at the time of her inglorious death. Like many young people she worked only as necessary, and always resigned when she had a few thousand in cash and the air fare to Bangkok. Though fully trained as a preschool teacher she preferred more casual, better paid work. Her recent occupations included heroin courier, prostitute, croupier at the Club 69 and layout artist for the advertising firm of Edward de Schizo, Copout and Lipschitz. Her parents refused to open the door to me – or rather, closed it when they perceived I was not the telegram boy they at first mistook me for – but her sister recalled her as a bright, cheerful, vivacious lass, fond of children and possessed of a lively mind and a compassionate nature. At the time of her death – through disembowelment, at the foot of the St Jude Station escalator, early Tuesday June 26 – she was living in a one-bedroom Euston apartment with Phoebe Cosgrove, the lady who conducts the weight-lifting classes at the Green Man Gym in Liverpool Street. I called by to see Phoebe, who also took me for a telegram boy – perhaps because of the pale-blue sports shirt I happened to be wearing at the time, together with my officious manner – but I've decided there was nothing important Phoebe could have told me anyway. Had the Ripper begun and finished with Phoebe's paramour, we'd have a problem, as the Hartebeest is well connected and does not keep the Black Book, as is common practice in most brothels. Happily, however, there were four further victims, the better for us to discern, and in all likelihood dismiss, an obvious pattern. From my own readings of psychopathic killers, they are nothing if not astute.

The Ripper's third victim was Owen Evans, forty-year-old co-proprieter of Aristotle's bottle shuttle in Montebello Road, but better known for a sword-swallowing act on the club circuit. His partner, always a handsome young man and he seemed to have no dearth of them, supplied the costumes for which the act was justly renowned, though I've heard it said a bit less attention to visuals and more to the musical accompaniment (which took the form of Joan Sutherland singing arias from *Lucia di Lammermoor* – recorded, she charges 10,000 big ones to do it live I believe) might have hastened his progress from prawn mornings to the Peppermint Grove children's parties to which he aspired. Though Evans can scarcely have been short of a quid – I'd hate to tell you what Sandy Scott wants for an evening at the Bowling Club (I chair the House Committee, so I know) – he had a blemished record, and was once caught attempting to smuggle snakes from Darwin in northern Australia. It's known half the passengers that leave that port have something up their trousers – snakes, goannas, geckos, turtles, anything that can be kept docile by packing it with ice-cubes supplied by the hosties – but Owen's ambitious ruse came to grief off the coast of Irian Jaya. He'd swallowed a four-foot taipan before boarding – they bring a phenomenal price in Hamburg – but had to drink so much whisky on the rocks to keep both the snake and himself comatose that he threw up in the toilet and couldn't get the snake back down his throat without the sound of Dame Joan singing. The snake had its neck broken in the process, so they booked him on a charge of threatening a threatened species and behaviour liable to cause a reasonable air traveller serious alarm and affront.

Now I've travelled to Britain in the company of a party of Australian international sportsmen, and had one of them swallowed a four-foot taipan it would have come as light relief.

Owen Evans was found disembowelled in a urinal opposite St Stephen's Hospital on June 28, just two days after the death of Myfynwy Milligan. Like me, he suffered from a weak bladder, specially in winter, and was in the habit of visiting the urinal every night on his way home from work.

I have established that both Evans and Milligan ate ghostloaves for breakfast and purchased dreggs rather than keep chooks. You don't need a big backyard for the purpose and it saves your table scraps going to waste.

June 25 and 27 I was doing the run. Shutter 63 began falling on August 29, but it also fell on May 22 at 12.22, when old Bottler had the colic. Fifty dollars for a visit from the vet, now there's public money well spent.

Somehow the police managed to keep the second and third murders quiet. Perhaps they didn't want to precipitate panic among the gay community. If the gay community panicked the socialites wouldn't be able to have their hair set, the Black and Blacker Ball would have to be cancelled and there'd be more derelicts on the winter streets, with a consequent upsurge in criminal activity.

The Black and Blacker Ball; that's a rort for people who don't know if their arseholes have been drilled, bored, punched or countersunk.

No, I haven't forgotten the Ripper's first victim, I'm saving him for last.

The first week of July was quiet. I was on the night shift. The search for eyewitnesses drew an eyepatch. No one would admit to having seen Owen Evans enter the urinal. Neither the police nor crime reporters later could imagine what Myfynwy Milligan was doing, standing on the escalator at St Jude Station late one night when she should have been at work. She was never known to travel by train and St Jude is not on the northern suburbs line.

Personally, I'm not the least surprised. Nothing the likes of Myfynwy Milligan did would surprise me in the least. People who've lost contact with the soil and the subsoil and who spend their childhood watching television are capable of behaviour bamboozling to an ordinary policeman. I remember Cadwalloper telling me how Balthazar Ganjadin got himself arrested for going into the ladies at the Art Gallery. When asked why he'd done such a thing he said he didn't know, but his mother told the PM and me on the quiet he'd seen something teeming with pregnant personal meaning in the form of an arrowhead on a work of modern art, which indicated all his personal problems – and God knows, he's got a few – would be resolved if he followed that arrow, heedless of the consequence. I don't know if the three days he spent in boob helped, but I do know he spends more time on his sculpture since the story got round, if you can call a colour-blind bowerbird's bower a piece of sculpture. He's fencing with Tindle, but how long before he refuses to fell some tree he likes the look of? He's got as much sense of direction as a blind-faced mail bundle.

Myself, I think a few young Constables Balthazars are much needed. They'd know at once why Myfynwy Milligan was miles out of her way. She probably saw a white dove by the War Memorial and followed it.

Here's a piece of police logic for you: was Myfynwy Milligan hurled from a train? No, because the guard would have seen it.

Now God knows, I don't want to criticize the guards of the State Rail Authority. Could a more boring, lonelier, colder, overpaid job be imagined? And there's always danger. What about the time Barry Bitterbest, who lives in that little brown house with the laurel windbreak on the Plymouth edge of Dog Rock, staggered from the pub with a sixpack of steam to catch his 2 p.m. bus home, with a stone train passing the ladies' rest room? The SM swears to this day he thought Barry was a goner. The driver was blasting his whistle so loudly he almost woke the observer. The SM ran out, knowing it'd be him who'd have to clean up the mess and they never find everything. (I was speaking to a shunter in the public bar of the Dog Rock hotel one night and he told me he once found a human heart stinking of methylated spirits impaled on the handbrake of a wheat hopper in the Rozelle marshalling yards.) Anyway, the driver hit the anchors so hard the guard got thrown twenty-five feet and had to be taken to hospital by ambulance. Old Barry just walked off, and he denied he'd even been downtown when the Sergeant spoke to him the next morning – no point talking to him at the time – and he's never spoken to the SM from that day to this one.

Some of the things these guards do hardly bear repeating, but I'll risk it: you know Norma Calvary who was on *The Price is Right*? She's got a tumour at the back of her neck. They tell me they've taken skin grafts, we don't know yet if it's malignant. Been there ten or twenty years according to the specialists, well, she's always been a scatterbrain, which may account for it. Poor old Alice her mother, at her age, with her sciatica and her cataract over one eye, how she manages we'll never know. She took in Jennie, that's Norma's youngest. Her father took her when he and Norma split up, and her stepmother wouldn't have her in the house when he died, ordered her out. Poor kid, she's just like her father, never says a word; not like her sister, who takes after Norma, won't shut up for five minutes. Now what I was going to say, she's not yet seventeen, yet she's going out with a guard of forty-five. Six kids older than she is. She goes in the guard's van with him, you can't tell me it's right. Norma went in to the booking office in Cosgrove Place to complain. Of course, poor Jennie, she's six foot six, it must be hard. Wanted to join the police force, and Cadwalloper says she should have been taken, should have been welcomed with open arms. These five-foot-eight striplings they're taking in are no good, he says, in a pub brawl: you need to know your back's covered. But all they said was she'd want a good pass in English in her Higher School Certificate.

60

Do you think she'll give this guard up? Alice went and saw his wife at Mount Woolfe. She claimed she put her husband's last girlfriend in hospital. Still, Jennie's got a mind of her own and at sixteen what can you do? I'm told the ladies' at the swimming pool is always filthier than the men's and the graffiti is worse.

As for noting a body thrown off a train, the SM was telling me the other day a wheat train went through here last week and turned up at the silos a hundred ton light. The guard had no explanation.

They've always been a bunch of rogues on the railways. Those that do the right thing are victimized by those that won't. When I arrived here the Dog Rock Station had the best display of cabbage and Cecil Brunner roses in green-painted forty-four-gallon drums I've seen. The tourists used to pick them as they returned from using the station lavatory on Sundays, before it was locked because of vandals. When they're doing the track up and have to use the refuge sidings, the SM comes in on a Sunday, when the station is normally unattended, to throw the points. He says you'd be amazed the class of people get off that train Sunday with no ticket. By law, their name and address must be noted.

They took his lad, they deprived him of his station assistant, so he pulled out those roses by the roots and threw them in an S-truck full of empty kegs while checking a passing express freight for hot axle boxes. He has no time to water and prune, with eighty trains going through a day.

They couldn't sack him for it. The only reprimand he's ever had was for failing to note the particulars when the Sunraysia overshot the platform one morning and Vince Izzard's mother got carried on. It wasn't till she mentioned it to the CWA meeting anyone thought to complain. They can't sack you from the SRA, it's like the public service. Loco driver Duncan Dropkick refused a transfer as it would have meant selling the family orchard, so now he's on the fettling gang at his old rate of pay. He's nearly sixty, won't lift a dog spike, and he gets more money than the ganger. They say there's a gang out Moolabah where the ganger's the only able-bodied man on the whole gang and the lowest paid. You can't tell me that's good for morale, and Australia Post is no better.

I broke one of my teeth last year, carrying the mailbags from the station. When I claimed for the X-ray I received a reprimand from some twenty-year-old spiky-headed clerk at the district office, saying, 'I view with concern the circumstances surrounding your recent accident. Any further breach of safe working practice by you will be regarded by me most seriously.'

I'd better not start on Australia Post. In the days of steam Dropkick Snr was a driver on a one-track line down south. It was common practice in those days to report in from unattended stations up to an hour ahead of time, so as to gain the fireman and the driver an hour's free run in the Railway Hotel. Being winter, they were full of rum and cloves one night and fell asleep in the cab with the fire on. Lost their water and the plug fell out of the boiler. Had to decommission the loco. Mrs Dropkick saw it being towed past her kitchen window by the breakdown gang as she was doing the washing up the next morning. The family lived in one of those little railway shacks two feet from the line where apple trees and peaches grow from pomes and cores thrown out of windows. There's still a few of them Cow Flat way: Wally Wilson from Ways and Works worked his way into one. She knew what it meant, so she clutched her many children to her ragged skirts, as her tears fell on the Sunlight soap, and she said to them, 'Children' she said, 'go to the haberdashery and with the last of the housekeeping money buy me a pair of rocket needles and a sack of twenty-ply wool, that I may sit by the coal fire late into the night, knitting coats for dairy cows, so you will all become dentists and judges, diplomats and doctors of philosophy.' Which is how she acquired those muscles in her upper arms. She's still alive, living with Dropkick. Still sitting by the fire. Cassandra Isbester, the doctor's wife, wants her to pass on her skills before she dies. Those coats fetch a great price in the city today, and she could knit one in twenty minutes. Essentially a Turk's-head knot with six holes, very intricate.

The Ripper's fourth victim, I hardly need mention, was Xavier Morgan, the famous personality. I don't know that Morgan had any talent, but he was very famous. His sonorous, authoritarian voice could boost the sales of any commodity, from margarine to prime movers. He sang country music for Kan Do. His rugged, clean-shaven face bespoke a certain self pride. There wasn't much Xavier didn't know and nothing he couldn't look up. Here was an embodiment of the Australian accent; witty, wealthy, well-connected, able to converse with politicians yet equally at home among thieves and rogues. Anyone in Mount Evatt with personal problems knew who to ring for the answer over the airwaves. As an actor, there was no element of Morgan's own personality he could not project convincingly, as many a local telemovie attests. As a famous lover, he found something to hanker for in every superannuated beauty queen he met: there was no sport he had not played, however badly, no TV current affairs programme he had not watched, no personal problem he had not experienced personally. He had a deep interest in exploration, and once chartered a helicopter to fly him over the dangerous Sepik River in New Guinea. Outside his Keating Point villa a host of people gathered on weekends, hoping to glimpse the great man as he buffed his Ferrari or tuned his Bugatti. Sometimes he strolled across to the fence to solve someone's personal problem for them. Yet was Morgan happy? We have it on his own authority he was not. Countless interviews betray his insecurity, his inconsolable melancholy. Tea-towels were downed in every Dog Rock household the night he appeared on the Mike Parkinson show and gave the most candid exposé of his tragic life since last year's interview in *Cleo*. He drove to work each morning in a different car and slept with a different woman each night, yet he was not happy. He had yet to find the perfect sports car, the perfect woman. Early each morning he rose from his sleepless bed – no drug on the market could sedate him more than an hour – and I don't think there was a dry eye in the studio audience as he told how he watched the sun rise over the city from the window of his lonely cupola, while praying to innumerable pagan deities to take him through another day. Here was a paradox, if you like: a man awarded the Order of Australia, doubtful of his own achievements. The biggest grazier east of Shark Bay, worried about his standing with the Deputy Commissioner for Taxation. A man who once hosted a television programme called *Xavier Morgan's Galactic Supercluster*, uncertain of his own cosmic significance. It was more than we could stand when the famous voice cracked and the tears rolled down the famous face. Ben Chuckyfried phoned in, offering the consolations of Gayleen. Mrs Topwaite sent her winning exhibit in the category 'Tall and Slender, Green and White' from the Uniting Church Horticultural Exhibition. Illyrius Hardacre of Bugloss Barren Grounds consigned his best A1-bred heifer under two years to Morgan's hobby stud. Dulce Dwyer finally parted with that pale blue crochet coathanger cover that's won its class at the Bonny Tops show every year since 1967 (best crochet coathanger cover, exhibitor over sixty-five years). I must confess I was on the point of sending Big Max, my prize-winning pumpkin, which only goes to show what watching television does to your grey cells. The postage alone would have cost me a week's wages.

On the evening of Wednesday July 11, an off-pension week – Sambo does the pensions – a cold night by Sydney if not by London standards, Xavier Morgan dined at the home of his business associate Gustav Gladhandle, a lobbyist and hobby farmer of Fitznev. Also present were Simon Scuttlecompo, a Toorak solicitor, his wife Deborah and her lover Phineas, and sundry poker machine manufacturers, racing identities and MLAs.

About midnight Morgan, in the company of Scuttlecompo and two young women who were not at the party, was seen dancing, after a fashion, under the lasers in the upstairs disco at the Eighteen Footer and Cloven Footed Club, Bottral Bay. They left at 2.05 a.m., Scuttlecompo driving a primrose Porsche Turbo and Morgan riding his MV Augusta motorcycle. As it has no pillion seat he rode home alone and without a helmet: he carried a doctor's certificate stating his head was too big to fit inside one.

The young lady turned up in a Black and White cab at the gates of his Keating Point Villa some half hour later. It is estimated Morgan would have made the journey on his MV Augusta in five minutes flat. The bell was rung, but there was no answer. Eventually, the butler came to the gate. He said he'd heard the bike arrive. A search of the house was followed by a search of the grounds. Morgan's body was found by the fence, cruelly disembowelled. In all likelihood, he'd seen someone there with a pressing personal problem and had gone over to provide the solution. He declined searchlights and armed guards on the gate as a concession to his long-suffering neighbours.

As soon as Morgan got within reach, the implement went through the railings and gutted him.

There was no keeping this out of the papers. Melbourne excepted, the nation mourned. All the murders came out. Builders' labourers everywhere walked off in the middle of concrete pours. Dishwasher sales soured. It was the way he died that so upset us; a martyr to the Good Life, slaughtered by psychopath.

The Queen's Park Ripper was now an entity known and feared the nation over, Melbourne excepted. But worse was to come. In the boldest stroke of his entire campaign, the Ripper struck again two nights later, July 13, a Friday. Flamboyant Barney Bolch-Corio, a judge of the family court, was struck down as he emerged from a seafood restaurant in Wellington Street. A shocking thing, this; one of the nation's most brilliant legal gut-thinkers, eviscerated. A QC who'd drawn his $1,500 a day at countless Royal Commissions of Inquiry into the habits of working-class criminals, reduced to a fishy-smelling corpse. His loss was mourned from one end of Brief Street to the other. He left a well-bred wife, a well-educated child, a Filipino housemaid and a collection of antique furniture so valuable and so heavy that no removalist would shift him from his home, which he'd socially outgrown, as it was situated at the far end of a Dunfegan driveway so wet and so steep that schoolboys are still finding bits of the Bechstein grand piano that five years ago got away from seven sturdy men, bolted down the drive, rocketed off a ledge, and overshooting completely the house, jungle and pool area of industrialist Sir Watto Urbanski – to the astonishment of the visiting French fencing team barbecuing by the pool – plummeted into a two acre nature reserve at the foot of the scarp, where it cut a swath twenty feet wide through the last remaining stand of red cedar in the whole of Middle Arm.

I think it was the same French fencing team our lads took on at the Cow Flat show. Someone, hearing there was a French fencing team in the country, arranged an exhibition match through the French Embassy. Our lads turned up in thongs and shorts, with post-hole diggers and chainsaws, and had their section of fence up and strung before the Froggies had even finished strapping on their protective gear. Seeing as how they was beat, some of the Froggies wanted a scrap, but the stewards were having none of it. Armed to the teeth, they were. Talking about it later in the pub, it was clear they'd known they were in for a hiding. Hadn't even brought any chainsaws with them, well I suppose they expected us to provide them. Always the same with these bloody wogs, expect the host to provide everything. Someone suggested that maybe French fences aren't the same as our own, but one of the older lads, who'd been through France *en route* from Lucerne to Calais by coach, said – and he was quite right – there'd have been no objection at all to a bit of stone fencing, the crowd would have lapped it up. Anyway, the Frogs went off in a huff, leaving us laughing at their stupidity.

How very depressing this is, reciting a list of murder victims. However, I've come to the lucky last in a lane off Corduroy Street, Friday August 10, Rubyfruit Rocqueforte, who with Sappho Cunynghame organized the Women against Rape in War and Sex with Men in General Protest that over the past year disrupted the Recitation of the Ode at countless rissoles throughout the state. The lights would dim as usual, the tables fall silent, the bar sales halt, speaking of which, if a licensed club doesn't aim for a 50 per cent gross profit from the bar it may as well put itself in the hands of the receivers. Lombard von Lumpsum, our Club Treasurer, former bank manager and husband of the current Madam President Viva von Lumpsum – which means to say Lombard doesn't know what goes on between the balance sheets – a man who once rode in the same lift as Malcolm Fraser and who last year in Suva had the privilege of buying a whisky and soda for a man, who though he strongly denied it, could only have been James Galway the Irish flautist – which is not to say von Lumpsum could whistle 'Annie Laurie' – and pokies by law must return 80 per cent to the player, which is not to say every player, on every occasion, gets just that: some get many times that amount. During my stint as Senior Vice President, which involves clearing the pokies as well as chairing the House Committee, which under our memorandum and articles of association monitors members' behaviour – and any letter of suspension I am obliged to recommend I always deliver, before the other mail, first thing Monday before the club opens – Alf Newcomer recently got six weeks for throwing up all over the curried egg sandwiches at the presentation night for the President's Triples, besides which I understand he often crawls home from the clubhouse on his hands and knees, the sort of thing that gives us a bad name, specially when he's wearing his DRBRC navy-blue blazer and hatband . . .

Blast. I've lost my thread. And there's that bloody phone again.

'Hello?'

'Sergeant wants to speak with you, D'Arcy D'Oliveres. Are you aware you left your filthy stinking tobacco in here?'

'So that's where it is. I'll be up to get it presently. Hello?'

'D'Arcy. I have to ask you to move those bees before they kill someone.'

'What! They've been in my yard seven years and have caused no trouble in all that time.'

'I believe they've stung Mrs Rochester on at least five occasions.'

'Yes, well they don't like motor mowers. I can't say I blame them. I gave her honey.'

'You can't buy your way out of this one, D'Arce. The town is convinced it was your bees killed Miss Hathaway's horses.'

'And what do you think?'

'You and Ursula Topwaite are the only beekeepers here and I went round to see hers yesterday and they're all dead, which surprised her greatly.'

'What! I should have been informed. What did they die of? If my bees come down with foulbrood . . .'

'They starved to death, as far as we could see. Besides, I'm informing you now. And I'm giving you one week to get those bees out of your backyard.'

'I'll speak to the district apiary officer over this.'

'Feel free. I've already spoken to him. Are you aware it is an offence to keep bees within a certain distance of a public road?'

'Oh yes, but . . .'

'Oh yes but nothing. It's a law seldom invoked, but I have to act on complaints, and I've had so many complaints D'Arce, the bees go. Now are you or are you not entering the State Pairs? How can I do my job as Bowls Secretary . . .'

'I'm not playing bowls with you anymore.'

'Oh for God's sake, D'Arcy!'

'I mean it. You've put my jack in the ditch for the last time. Those bees mean a lot to me. You wouldn't understand.'

'I'm not asking you to get rid of them. Just move them out of town.'

'I've nowhere I can put them. Do you seriously think I'd stoop so low as to kill horses using bees as proxies?'

'I don't know. I'm not a beekeeper. But everyone in this town knows how you like animals, D'Arce.'

'Bees are animals.'

'You're suspected of having shot Mrs Pobjoy's Persian tomcat. You don't deny you fractured the skull of Jennings' red cattle dog. You make no secret of what you think of brown-coloured sheep and Kashmir goats. Now you're on nights this week, so you shift those bees, you hear me? And have I had your last word on the State Pairs, Mr Senior Vice President?'

'I won't be playing with you. Put me down with Arblaster. And let me give you a word of advice: never use your drive shot unless you've got backwoods, son. Good day.'

As I'm going abroad I'd better see Arblaster. He may prefer to play singles. I seldom seek the man out, as I find his views on the state of the world depressingly negative. But let me just get my tobacco and I'm going straight out to Idle-a-While. Though not himself a beekeeper, Bert is the one man in Dog Rock who will understand my feelings at this moment.

4 Fancy selling the dairy to Dr Isbester. When I first set eyes on Isbester he was heading towards the public bar of the Dog Rock hotel wearing an old blue boilersuit and a knitted beanie of the kind favoured by metalworkers in cold climates. I'd put his age at fifty-six. I hear he knows a lot about Light Sussex cockerels, but I've never pursued the subject with him because of his unpleasant manner: he makes a practice in the Post Office of laughing at every word I utter, while staring straight at the nearest pretty female for approbation. I guess he's the son of an attractive mother who never had much time for him, and I think had I been his stepfather I'd have treated him pretty badly as well: it's hard enough tolerating a stepson who can do even one thing properly and Isbester can do every bloody thing, as he never tires of demonstrating.

He bought most of Labour-in-Vain, including the part Arblaster swore he wouldn't sell to his worst enemy, which would have to be Rick Cotter the milkman or possibly Alf Calvary the patriarch. I'm pretty sure old Bert keeps a noddy log. Every grievance against the neighbours is entered, towards the inevitable showdown. Though we haven't had the showdown, we must have come close the morning Alf parked in Bert's spot at the club. That log has been handed down over a hundred years now, and I dare say it's as fat as a retail tobacconist. I reckon it'd be a good week's work just reading it out over the fence.

You know, I hate to see an old retired farmer wearing a brand new pair of reading spectacles. It makes me sorry for his wife.

It's swamp, you see, paperbark country. Wearing whiskers on the map. I had the map out yesterday, plotting a two-mile radius from Hathaway's stables, when I happened to notice on the key, just above the whiskers that mark a permanent swamp, a series of lazy Fs that mark a rice paddy. Isbester should have called the place the Lazy F, as that's what Bert reckons he is, and he fully intends to grow rice on it. Was a time we'd have laughed at this, but I reckon the ashram has changed that. Do you know they've been bringing in pawpaws to sell at the greengrocer's all winter?

Silly Isbester went out and married a thirty-five-year-old bird. He kept Bert on as manager, and Bert says his balls are bigger than his brains but oh

Woo!

Gut's gone to water . . . ulcer's playing up . . . worry of the bees . . . must get onto it straight away. Serepax! Tagamet! Only a couple of weeks now to the jellied eel.

.

Whew, that's better. Now where's my script gone? I'm sure I put it here with the cats' toys. Here's one. '*Recipe.* Sod. phenobarb. gr. 1/4, Mist. Gent. Alc. ad.oz.VIII, Tinct. Card. Co. minums 10', no no, that's the script that ancient old locum wrote me just before he died. Nordette nearly died too when she saw it – that's Nordette Pruvagol, our pharmacist. Said she hadn't made a mixture of gentian and cardamom since World War II. This'll be what I'm looking for, 'Stematil mg 5, Mitte 25, Typhoid vacc. 2 amps' no . . . Ah! This must be it. 'Serepax mg 15, Mitte L, Tagamet 150, Sig 1 tds & nocte'. Opfinger had to apply to the National Health for the Tagamet. Very expensive, but you can't keep drinking Mylanta, it's like a barium meal. I think that's what's wrong with my septic: the pump on Jennings' old truck is just not strong enough to pull the aluminium. Can you make out if there's one repeat or two? Paxyl Opfinger, write more clearly.

When Nordette first came here there were those who thought she wouldn't succeed. I'm sure sales of Wet-cheks went down initially. Old Tuss had let the place go to pieces. All he had in one window was a rack of Happy Baby Soothers, a display of Woodward's Gripe Water, some Fisherman's Friend lozenges covered in dust and a bottle of Spencer's bronchitis mixture replaced each spring by a packet of Fabahistin. Nordette changed all that. She got rid of the rubbish out of the other window too, all those old bottles labelled 'Glyc. Ac. Carb.', 'Ol. Bergam.', 'Pulv. Ulm. Ful.' The mortar and pestle went. And now you wouldn't know the place. Both windows chockablock with Boots Number 7 depilatory creams, Revlon blushers, Rubenstein eyeshadow, Brut, Old Spice, Mennen, Tabac – if sales of Rendells Pessaries and Koromex haven't kept pace I'd be most surprised. The young mums of the district know where to come for their Nappysan now, and while they're waiting for junior's Septrin suspension and Paracetemol they can choose a lipstick from a range of colours you wouldn't wear to the Hammersmith Odeon. There's a nailcare centre, a sunglasses stand, a barrel of shampoos on special – she employs both Rayleen Addiboy and that spiky-headed piece from Cow Flat that hangs round with Big Owl. I reckon she's a credit to us. So what if she lives in Bonny Tops? She knows so much about us she wouldn't want to mix here socially.

That bloke's a traveller, 11.45 a.m. Travellers never call after 3 p.m. What becomes of travellers after 3 p.m. is one of Life's little mysteries, like how all the high school kids catch their bus when there's never anyone waiting.

I can see Nordette in the dispensary. She'll be typing up a bottle of Brufen for the old battleaxe next to the Quellada stand. Headlice are a problem at the school this term.

'Good morning, D'Arcy. Didn't see you in Church Sunday, were you unwell?'

'To tell you the truth, Mrs Orloff, I'm suffering terribly from ulcers. But the town's communications with the outside world must be maintained.'

'Is something on your conscience? Miss Hathaway says to tell you that *God* is *Love.*'

'Yes, well I did my bit for the African missionaries, Mrs Orloff. Which is more than some can say.'

'It's the Men's Group Ladies Night tonight, D'Arcy. We're hoping to see you along. Inspector Truelove will be showing us his slides of Disneyland and The Grand Canyon.'

'Oh, what a shame, I believe I've seen them twice already. You know, I never wanted to be churchwarden: I feel hardly worthy of the honour. And I think Miss Pruvagol is trying to attract your attention.'

'It's you I want to speak to, D'Arce. Here's your prescription, Mrs Orloff. And don't forget, no matter how stiff you feel, only one three times a day. D'Arcy, is it true you're going down to Mr Arblaster's when you leave here?'

'That is correct, yes.'

'Be a dear and take this to him.'

'I'd do anything for you, Miss Pruvagol. Good Lord, he's not going to eat all these is he?'

'To tell you the truth, I'm most concerned at the dosage he's on. I think his doctor is acting very irresponsibly. He gets a carton like this three times a week and it's all on the NHS. I've been prescribing for cardiac cases since I was twenty-two and I've seen nothing like it. He's on both Serepax and Anginine, prndu. Do you know what that means?'

'When necessary, as directed.'

'Oh, you do know what it means. You're a clever man for a postman. I'd hate to see Mr Arblaster's heart. He takes enough Anginine to kill a horse!'

'Please, Miss Pruvagol – could I ask you to make up my own prescription now?'

'I'm sorry, D'Arcy, I can't make this up, it's four months old. You'll have to see your doctor.'

'Why should I have to see bloody Opfinger every time I need Tagamet? I know what's wrong with me!'

'I don't make the rules, D'Arcy. He might write you a script over the phone.'

'No, I don't think so. He'll never own his own hobby stud if he does that. He'll say to me, "It's a while since we've seen you, D'Arcy, better take your blood pressure".'

'I think you should have your blood pressure taken. You've gone quite purple in the face.'

'Have I now? And what's the treatment, Miss Pruvagol? Perolysen? Catapres? More money for May and Baker and Boehringer Ingelheim? More money for Paxyl Opfinger. More money for the Medicare scribes? What about some social justice, eh?'

'You talk to your mate Albert about social justice. I'm busy.'

'Very few of us would be ill if there was such a thing as social justice.'

I shouldn't have spoken to her like that, her of all people. I hate myself for it now. It's just the thought of parting with those fifteen bucks I can ill afford. Buy a couple of bottles of duty-free Red Label Johnny Walker with those.

Shutter 63 hasn't fallen again. I was expecting as much.

See those birds? Cruise missiles? Eastern rosellas, gold and blue. The crimson rosellas are royal blue and red. They fly a bit higher and eat cotoneaster berries. Both are predominantly seed feeders and only sit in trees to look around. Birds of the same genus are brightly coloured when they share a habitat: you see it among human beings in Queens Park. Two of the most beautiful species of parrot in the world yet common as dirt. One thing you don't get back home, eh. Pheasants were my favourites there but they're as English as rhododendrons. These birds are Australian.

Sometimes, when I wonder what I'm doing here, I just go out and look at the birds. I've identified 133 species from my back verandah. Dog Rock is the junction of so many habitats, within two miles of Hathaway's stables we have rainforest, dry sclerophyll, open farmland, scattered woodland, marsh, on top of which lots of migrants pass through on their annual journeys. I love to see the spine-tailed swifts swooping in the autumn sky as they make their way back to the northern hemisphere via Singapore.

A great place for birds, but a wretched place for butterflies. I think I've added only fifteen species to my collection since I've been here. If you see me suddenly leap from the car, by the wayside, it's because I've spied a female Orchard Swallowtail. They seem to boycott my lemon tree and I only see them when I've too much mail to stop. The ones I've caught have been slightly marked. By the end of summer they're torn to shreds on the thorns of the Eureka lemons.

There's a nice little butterfly in the park, the Swordgrass Brown, or is it Brown's Swordgrass? Many of the local plant species were first described by a man called Brown. I'd have liked to have met him. One of the wattles in the park is called Acacia brownii, and I was pointing it out to a pair of hikers once when one of them turned to the other and said, 'Oh yes; the flowers look just like little arseholes, see?' One of the satyrs, the Swordgrass Brown. I know exactly where to find it. It hovers near the drains next to a track by Calvary's Lookout. A butterfly reminds me of happiness: you think in the beginning you can catch it with your bare hands but you wind up chasing it with a bloody great net.

I'm not much of a collector. I learned that last year. I walk in the park to keep fit for hiking and I'd spent the weekend away. I was in a place I'd never seen before, chasing some lyre bird or other. The sort of place you expect to find a Maclean's Swallowtail if anything. Suddenly I looked up, and there, in the sunlight on the mottled trunk of a coachwood, was the most beautiful butterfly I have ever seen. It was the colour of a Mountain Blue, that haunting, bright, iridescent blue, but as big as a Cairns Birdwing. It had owlets down the sides of its upper wings that reminded me of a Grey Pansy, but the edges of its lower wings were the deep brown velvet of the Two Brand Crow. I think it was new. I'm pretty sure I could have attained immortality through it. God, was my heart pounding as I reached up – I had no net – and it just let me take it and I held it, pulsing, in my hands. I must have stood there quite some time before I let it go.

Right, we're coming to the Arblaster estate. If you've never seen fuschias, prepare yourself. Just behind that windbreak is Isbester's prize-winning home. We were all dreading what it might look like. Mudbrick sort of place, we imagined, but no, the learned doctor designed it himself and handed the plans to a local, Amos Jennings, who couldn't make head nor tail of them. With Michael Muckelthwart the brickie, he spent three wet weeks in the club pouring over the plans. Eventually, a move had to be made. The subbie who excavates Jennings' jobs, Hardacre from Barren Grounds, got his dozer bogged so many times getting on and off the site, that Amos told the doctor he'd have to put a road in if he wanted his bricks within half a mile.

Mother drives the Merc see, and he's in his little four-wheel-drive Suzuki.

'Just dump'em by the gate is best,' says he. 'I'll be doin' the labourin'. Ask young Mike if he's any objection to workin' another brickie. When I'm labourin' I feed two, and I use me own larry.'

The building inspector was supposed to come out before the footings were poured, but as it was raining he gave Amos a ring. 'Everything okay?' 'Yes.'

You can be lucky or you can be unlucky. Time will tell. No inspector in his right mind should have passed that site, in the middle of a slip. Amos says that while the clay stays wet the house stays up, but come drought, stand clear. One of the worst jobs Michael's ever done, there was no service pole and he had to rely on the radio in his ute. Did three batteries in. He tells me that when he was rigging stringlines over the footings before laying the first course – Isbester, true to his word, carted all the bricks over (on his back), and had them round the site ready to start at 7 a.m. (mudboard, stack of bricks, mudboard, stack of bricks) Michael reckons he kept the mud knocked up all day and he stickraked the beds and the perps and when he found himself a quiet moment he wrote scientific papers – by the time Mike had finished the last profile the first was out again, so he just shut his eyes and went ahead. When Amos came back to put the bearers on the piers there wasn't one pier plumb with another. 'Put'em on anyway is best,' says Isbester. 'You're the boss,' says Amos. Michael was dreading knocking the piers down and cleaning the bricks by hand. Convict-built bricks, they were. Like most brickies, Michael's euchred his back and his fingers are covered in birdseyes.

Now on a normal brick veneer the studs and trusses come on a truck. They're prefabricated, with the doors and windows in position. The tiler's working while the brickie is still putting up the outside walls, over the ant-capping under the dampcourse. But when Michael finished building the walls he found he'd bricked up the windows, and the top course, in six of the seven walls, was three feet out from the studs. 'No problem,' says Isbester. 'We'll just extend the ties.'

'Now listen,' says Jennings, thinking of his reputation. 'If you go on, you do it yourself.' So Isbester pulled all

76

the studs out and made a fire to warm the site and said to Mike, 'We'll make the house smaller, and then we'll have enough bricks for cavity walls throughout, which is best anyway.'

Now when you're building cavity walls you build half way up on the outside then half way up on the inside and your internal walls have to be tied in, otherwise they'll crack where they've been batted up. But Michael wanted the work and he was learning a lot about medicine, so he went ahead. He was dreading the final inspection. The bearers and the joists are supposed to be inspected but they're not, if the builder knows the inspector.

Before the roof could go on, we had that month of heavy rain and the walls got a bit of a lean-on. There wasn't a square wall in the whole house, and yet, by some miracle, the top courses finished up plumb, or pretty near. Overjoyed by this, Isbester went to town with his carpentry set, improvising a clutch of lofts inside the galvanized iron roof. There's not a window in the whole house, it has no plumbing or electricity, but before the building inspector could see it it won an award for contemporary design, so there wasn't much he could do after that, except order its demolition. I expect the legal wrangle to go on for years. In the meantime, Arblaster has the only view of the Masterpiece in town. His wife tells me he sits on the verandah and stares at it for hours on end.

Here we are then, Labour-in-Vain. Strictly speaking, Idle-a-While, but the mail still comes to Labour-in-Vain. I'll open the gate, there's a knack to it. This is a proper letterbox. I wish he'd donate all his hundreds of old milk-cans to the African Mission opportunity shop for sale as letterboxes. Get Dirk D'Oilycart to cut a slit in the base, weld a bit of pipe to the side and the result in a letterbox superior to any available commercially. I can fit a *National Geographic* in there. And who wants their Franklin Mint catalogue creased, so it sits up on the table like Jackie? If I were delivering, say, an implement, I'd hop off the bike here, reach over the fence, pop the

77

lid off the can and Bob's your uncle. But this is one box on the beat we can safely dismiss with assurance: Fargo's clocked it on the bike and it's 0.1 over the limit. Anything the least bit bulky or heavy stays at the PO when he's on the run. Old Arblaster comes in to pick up his carded parcels frothing at the dentures. He slams the cards down on the counter and if it weren't for the anginine tablet under his tongue he'd give the PM a good tongue-lashing. Strictly speaking, Fargo's right, so there's nothing the PM can do.

Will you look at that display of fuschias? Miniskirt, Knockout, Geisha Girl, Forward Look, Archie Owens, First Love, Maorie Maid, Corsair . . . if you think this is something, wait till you see the display by the Hacienda Blankety Blanca, which is what Bert calls the new dairy since Cassandra Isbester had it remodelled as a Spanish-style hospice for itinerant scholars of horsepiss. All the appropriate fuschias grace the entrance: Santa Clara, Boliviana, San Jose, Montezuma, San Leandro, Silverado, Linda Ronstadt, Tropicana . . . when I compare this place to the manager's cottage up the road where the Balthazars live like pigs in their pigsty with a garden that looks like a railway embankment, I worry for the future. I will say this for them though, they've built a polythene greenhouse in which to grow tomatoes and anyone who grows his own tomatoes can't be all bad.

A word of warning: don't mention the word 'milk'. Arblaster's allergic to it. It's a long story.

Someone's coming, it'll be her. The only time she can get anything done is when he's not here. Won't lift a finger. It'll see us out, he says. Good enough for my mother. Last time he went to the travel agency she tried to shift that rotten old Welsh dresser to the shed by herself. You can see where it went through the balustrade.

'Ah Mrs Arblaster. Bert home?'

'My Bert's always home when he's not playing bowls. When last I saw him he was standing in my kitchen warming his kidneys by the fuel stove before putting twenty-four imaginary bowls down the hallway before lunch. You coming in?'

'Just for a minute. Hello Bert! I see your big side-board's got the borers.'

'Ar blast your eyes you bloody useless blue-coloured rogue of a nosy postman. How can you wear shorts in this weather? And what have you got for me now? If it has windows it's old-fashioned. Or have you come here to tell me there's been a nuclear war and the Kashmir goats are out and eating the pine plantations? Cup of tea for the postie, Mother. Just put the carton down there, D'Arce.'

'How's your heart, Bert?'

'Ar blast me heart, if a man spent all day whingeing about his heart he'd have no time to whinge about other things. Did you see that bloody great hole in the road outside my front gate? Some little darlin's pony could break its leg there, but it should be fixed all the same. Where's that pepper-and-salt gang got to? Seen'em lately?'

'Friday last they were up Sandilands Place.'

'They're always up there. Bloody Cockburn with his four teenage daughters, they tell me they're coming and going up that street all night long. That Kirsty Cock-burn, she's a bold hussy of a thing. When she's tying her shoelace you can see what she had for breakfast. Big purple thighs on her like ledger books. She's going out with that Izzard lout isn't she? If he called by for my daughter driving that bloody great bed on wheels . . .'

'Here's your tea, Dad. Why don't you two go out on the verandah so I can get some work done?'

'Got time for a look at the Masterpiece, D'Arce? That's not a camera you've hidden there is it? No photos without permission.'

'Do you remember that Clean Phil Van Effendonk used to come through here years back, D'Arcy, I think he married one of those Beaudesert girls from Barren Grounds. Had that place in the granite country back of McSweeney the copper's son. Worst sheds and the worst fences and dirtiest paddocks I've ever seen. No man on earth could have carried away the junk he had around his sheds and house inside a month. Real hoarder. Never heard of Frenock. Anyway, Dirk's got his truck up the garage and Isbester's going to buy it. I said, you buy that you're buying trouble, but the doctor knows best.'

'Need a truck do you, Bert?'

'Ever heard of a grazier without a truck? See, what normally Dirk would dump at the tip we're taking to fill the drains.'

'Oh.'

'Isbester must be an intelligent man, D'Arcy, but he's a fool. He's as old as I am, but he's nicking with that young bird and he's knocked a foal out of her and he thinks he's young again, but have I got news for him. It's a good arrangement though, D'Arcy, it suits them both. He stuffs himself to death and she gets his money when he does.'

'And what's he like around the farm?'

'Absolutely hopeless. Can't anticipate the way an animal's going to move. He's up here most weekends now since he started his Brahmin breeding programme. She grows the rice. I said, you'd better electrify your fences. When those Indians see that rice they'll be through that fence like a packet of salts. He was here last Sunday with that Mr Justice Safehouse who buggered my chainsaw. Big, useless, red-faced, purple-nosed lawyer got a place out Cow Flat. I said, do you know how to use it? Oh yes, he says, use them all the time. When it came back there were chunks out of the teeth, the bar was blue and the chain was blue. I gave him a spare chain too, but I was lucky there: he couldn't unravel it. I said, it's just as well you blokes are good doctors and judges cause you'll never make farmers while your bums point at the ground. Mal'll say to me, which cow is that? That's your best cow, I say. Ten minutes later he'll say, now which cow is *that?* That's your best cow again, I say. I mean, you'd think he could learn to recognize the ear tags. He's only got three cows. And how are things with you, D'Arcy? Caught the Ripper yet?'

'I don't think they'll ever catch him, Bert. He's a canny bugger. The only clue is that implement and God knows what that might be. Bert, can I put my bees on your place? If I move them straight down by the top fence they'd be a mile from where they are now.'

'Fine by me, D'Arcy. They should do quite well off Miss Hathaway's blackberries and Paterson's curse. One thing I'll say for those Kashmir goats Safehouse runs, they eat the blackberries. A shame they eat the trees as well. No, that's fine by me. What, you've been given your marching orders have you?'

'Someone spread a rumour round town that my bees killed Miss Hathaway's horses.'

'You sure they didn't? I'd hate to see someone else's bees getting credit for what your bees did.'

'I can't see why they would, Bert. Bees only sting to protect their own stores and brood. In the field they'll sting in self-defence, but if you want my opinion it was Ursula Topwaite's bees. An absconding swarm, made up of starving bees, is a sight different to an ordinary one. They'd have had to have been desperate to swarm in September. She must have robbed them of every drop of honey they had. They're all gone, you know.'

'Well spread a counter-rumour then! You know more about bees than she does. She knows nothing about anything, that woman. What about the time . . .'

'The trouble is, Miss Hathaway's phone was ringing and I never answered it, Bert. It was ringing half an hour. The reason I never answered was the shutter had been falling since 29th August and keeping me awake half the night.'

'Faulty line eh?'

'I don't know. Pocock can find nothing wrong with it. Doesn't seem to be shorting out. And it never fell once on Sambo.'

'Don't mention that bastard to me. I'd like a karri tree to fall on him! Who does he think he is, driving round town in that Hudson? Dirk was saying there's not a part for that vehicle in the whole of this country. I reckon he'd be behind all this, D'Arcy. I reckon he wants to drive you out of town to make sure of his own job. One of you's going when the exchange closes and no one else'd feed him, he's nought but a bloody drone. You get my vote,

D'Arce, your pollen sacks are always filled with padded postal bookbags. Stick with it, D'Arcy! I tell you, it's a shocking thing to lose your manual exchange. A manual exchange fulfils a vital role in a town like this. I've known other towns lose their exchange and when it's gone, things deteriorate. The only people want an automatic exchange are those with something to hide. This Cassandra Isbester, she goes into Bonny Tops when she wants to use the phone to ring a certain person. I know of others do the same thing. There'll be more playing up than ever we've seen in our entire lives when that exchange goes, boy! When's it due to shut?'

'Maybe six months. By the way, before I forget, do you feel like playing men's pairs with me? I'm taking six weeks' holidays soon, which includes two weeks' long service, and I might play cricket yet, but the men's pairs are on Sunday mornings and I can get along to the Wednesday pairs one week in two as well – pension mornings, unfortunately – but I won't be playing men's fours while the cricket's on. And I never play mixed triples.'

'Neither do I! The last time I played mixed triples I copped that Viva von Lumpsum. They say the strongest queen in a hive stings her rivals to death. But I thought you always played with the Sergeant. Got to Country Week last year didn't yers?'

'I don't want to play with him. If there's one thing annoys me as a skipper it's having a number three who thinks he knows how I should bowl. The only shot he's got is his drive and he never knows when to use it. When he was my second he was forever watching the next rink. I always had to call him to the mat. And when he leads and you call for a long end he puts that jack in the ditch every time. Jack-in-the-ditch, we should call him.'

'You don't really need a copper in a town with a manual exchange. What's he do all day? Couldn't catch a combine harvester in a 3.3 litre Falcon. God help us if we ever had a crime here! They're supposed to practise with their service pistols every three months but it's more like three years, to save ammo. That's the government's fault. Couldn't hit the arse end of a hayshed, some of them. All he does is spray foxes with a spotlight and a twenty-two. It's the curse of the countryside, D'Arcy, the fox-shooting copper. That's the beauty of the Queensland gates up north: no copper on earth can work out how to open them. Oh, here's the missus back. Lunch up love?'

'You're not getting your lunch yet. You've been into my biscuits all morning. D'Arcy, I wonder could you spare us a pot of honey if we paid you for it? We bought a tin from Terry Derry's stall the other week and it's *dreadful!*'

Terry Derry's a pro. Like Arblaster the dairyman he owes his livelihood to the fact that certain natural products, beeswax and butterfat among them, are soluble in hot water but not in cold. Were it otherwise, the washing up would stretch to Kingdom Come. Apis mellifera, like Homo sapiens, was able to move from the tropics to the temperate regions thanks to his habit of nesting in cavities. The local Aborigines nested in cavities but they couldn't boil water, so Terry Derry is probably the first beekeeper to work these Dog Rock forests.

I want to visit that stall, but first, we'll pay a visit to the Balthazars. Malbane didn't get his dole cheque last week, so I reckon he'll be driving for the Bonny Tops Cab Co. He's got a three-class licence and he must have forgotten not to mention it when he filled in his last application. They're at home; I can hear Dodgecastle's guitar.

Some local people don't like Balthazars, but I don't mind them myself. A strong colony with plenty of stores can tolerate a few drones over winter. They keep the workers entertained with their clumsy antics.

By the way, did you notice how Arblaster's got a fair bit of social insect theory mixed in with his herd view of the world? And yet he's never kept bees. If he had, he'd have known straight off I couldn't put my bees down here. I'd have to move them somewhere else first. They must be moved at least three miles or the foragers keep flying back to the old site. Perhaps his father kept bees. Most dairymen did in the old days.

Ah, I hear the famous bass drum now! He's a bit of a one-man band, this lad. You'll see at least five photos of that bass drum in every issue of the *Bonny Tops Post*. People are always standing in front of it receiving trophies and big wooden spoons, but it's up on the stage and they're down on the floor so it pretty well dominates the setting. I seem to recall it has no front skin, and folded inside for some reason is the tartan blanket Mrs Worrywart gave to the V de P last winter, under the mistaken impression it would end up warming some needy person's knees. She was furious, seeing how Dodgecastle's the only son of the Dodgecastle in Dodge-castle, Nancarrow, Nonnemacher and Nosworthy, the merchant bankers.

Miss Hathaway's cable runs through that paddock. Dig it up, expose it to moisture; that's enough to short out the shutter. And a pressure pack you buy at the garage dries it out again. Telecom, learning Isbester was a doctor, had his phone on within three weeks. Miss Hathaway took advantage of it. Arblaster's still waiting for his. That's the reason we're making these calls.

Look at the old aviary. They've got a fig tree growing inside, I like the idea there. They're using it to keep the currawongs *out*. Those will be the only ripe figs ever seen in Dog Rock. That's the beauty of the persimmon: you can pick it when it still tastes like a penicillium mould and even the currawongs can't come at it.

Care for a peep at the lads' greenhouse? That should save us knocking on the door.

'Hey postie! Over here! Something for us? This way, mate.'

'Mr Malbane, isn't it?'

'That's right. How did you know?'

'How do you like driving the cabs?'

'Oh, don't mention it, please. You know what I took last night?'

'Let me see if I can guess. What's today? Tuesday. Monday night then, all right: assuming you started at

3.30 p.m. you'd have picked the cab up at the depot, filled up at the Golden Fleece and gone straight to the Bonny Tops rank. Between then and 5 p.m. you'd have opened the boot a fair few times for shopping trollies and seen a lot of the pickups at the Half Case and the Safeways. You'd have done a U-turn or two before a variety of weatherboard cottages, including one with a giant butterfly pinned to the shutters at 45 degrees. Dollar fifty plus waiting time. You'd have picked up Johnno, the steward at the Golf Club, at 5.30 precisely, and taken him out to work from the Ash Street flats. Three dollars fifty, on the account. On the way there he'd have asked you to make a booking to bring him home again, despite the fact he's the only person uses a cab after midnight Mondays, and if it weren't for his having lost his licence Horrie would have had to take another cab off the road. By this stage, you're probably the only cab on. You take Miss Holstein from the furriers to the top pub club lounge at 5.30 as well. Dollar fifty but no tip: because of Johnno you've kept her waiting. You meet the train at 5.47 but it's always twenty minutes late.'

'You've driven cabs yourself, mate!'

'No, but I know others have. Come sunset, there's a half hour's action as the licenceless alcos head off to the watering holes. They always come good when that sun goes down. Donny Bonomi from the Railway Camp perchance – sideburns, cowboy shirt, beergut, string ties – he'll surprise you by hailing the cab rotten drunk and asking to be taken not from, but to, the sportsman's bar at the bottom pub. He'll quiz you concerning the female drivers on the day shift. Cliff Beaudesert to the Bowling Club, two big dollars' worth. At 7.45 you take Danny Dooley the welder home from the top pub. Depending on how drunk he is, he may offer to chop all your wood for you. Captain Johnny Leftwich next, the diesel mechanic – towelling hat, no socks – home to Economos Drive, fifth telegraph pole on the right.'

'Gee, mate, how do you do it?'

'It's easy, once you get the knack. Maybe an hour or two on the rank now, doing nothing, before they all come staggering out, clutching the mandatory box of cans – pastry-cooks and housepainters in platform heels and flared trousers, dairyhands with their shirt tails out and their free elbow in the characteristic forward position that comes from a lifetime of lumping heavy buckets, curly-headed fitters in bib-and-tucker overalls – sometimes they laugh, sometimes they're crying. Pugnose from the pepper-and-salt gang would sell his soul for a pizza. And the fare? Fares don't matter any more. Slow as a bee frame, out comes, in triumph, the fistful of notes as the coins spill in the gutter. Take as much as you want, everyone else has. What you took last night was entirely up to you, son, *entirely* up to you. May I come in?'

'Sure. Dodger, have you met the postie? He'll be here in a minute. Can I be of help?'

'The C of E Men's Group is holding a Ladies Night tonight and I was wondering if either of you lads would care to show your slides of Nepal.'

'Ah, but I won't be here.'

'What? Horrie's got you driving Tuesday nights as well as Mondays! He must have seen you coming.'

'It won't be for long mate; I promise you that.'

'Here's the man himself: *you* wouldn't care to show your slides of Nepal to some ladies at the Church hall this evening?'

'I'd love to, but the band's rehearsing.'

'Never mind. Some other time perhaps. It's nice to know there's a local band that actually rehearses, though you wouldn't think so to hear it. Good day.'

No swelling about the face or wrists. Those two weren't stung yesterday.

The Dolly's River Bush Band would be the best bush band hereabouts. They're all losers and they sing losers' music for indigenous losers, though I must admit that when Renee sings 'Satin sheets to lie on, satin pillows to cry on' the way she did at the last Masonic Debutante's Ball, she conveys precisely the image of a Jody single bedroom suite in vinyl Kentucky walnut simulate.

They've got that giant, Kenny Gaff from Ben's Electrical, playing acoustic guitar, and he holds it like a ukelele. He must have learned guitar on a conventional strap and he holds it tightly under his chin. I thought he'd bring the house down when he sang 'My mother died of fright when she saw me in the light' but I don't know where Balthazar fits into it. A bit of a comedown, I should have thought, for a man who once put an ad in the local *Post*, saying 'Have your lawns mowed by your intellectual superior'. Oh well, let's get to the honey stall, Isbester and his missus won't be up till next weekend. He'll be bragging to the hospital registrars about how well his winter oats have done and she'll be tanning her tits at Oilskin Cove.

By Jove, the blackberries should do well if this weather holds up. It's funny, but I've never seen the local birds eat blackberries. King parrots – the ones that sound like squeaky gates – eat acorns. Galahs eat wheat off the railway track, satin bowerbirds eat French beans, silver-eyes eat elderberries, gang gangs eat hawthorns, black cockatoos eat Monterey pinecones – it's a habit by no means confined to the primates. Derry's stall is on the Plymouth side of town. He runs it on the honour system.

So what did you think of the manager's cottage? When the manager moved out he took the lino off the kitchen floor. He was really only a dairyhand. Arblaster gave him the push for losing all the herd records going back fifty years, when he accidentally burned down the old dairy. They were written on the slabs in chalk. Anything he left behind was fit for the tip. That old horsehair sofa, how can they bear the stench of it? It was out in the paddock twelve years. Had the saltlick on it.

Let's go over the whole shemozzle while we drive. Every single murder was committed on nights I was doing the run. I lower the flag at 4.20 p.m. and I could be in Queens Park by 8 p.m. if I had to. I have no alibi. After I clear the pokies at the club I go home, feed the chooks, feed the ducks, feed the cats, feed myself, and settle down in front of the boob tube with a book. I may attend a Church function or a meeting of the Club House Committee and if there's a good film at the drive-in I'll sometimes go to that. But of the six murders, two were committed on Wednesday night and two were committed on Friday night, and I never go out on either of those two nights, and one was committed on Monday night, another night I never go out, and the first murder occurred on the night of Tuesday 29th May and it differed from the others in more ways than that.

You know, that first murder's got me worried.

Tuesday night is the favoured night for holding meetings in Dog Rock. It's the best night for TV viewing, so the meetings don't drag on. Everyone's anxious to be home by 8.30 p.m. at the latest.

Frankly, these meetings are a waste of my precious time, and there's no way I'll be standing for office next year or any other year. I reckon I've done my bit. I think the only local committees I haven't served on are the CWA, the Brownies, the Women's Hockey Club and the RSL Auxiliary. I've been Bowls Secretary, Bible Secretary, President of the Basketball Association, though I've never played basketball – I was responsible for changing the name of the local side from '69'ers' to 'Ball Bashers' – junior vice captain of the Dog Rock Bush Fire Brigade, patron of the Swimming Club, though I can't swim out of sight on a dark night, and treasurer of the Cricket Club. I've run the Scouts, the Red Cross, the P&C, the Parents without Partners (and God knows how I got roped into *that*). I've chaired meetings of the local Community Development Association and plotted to fill the hotel in summer. I've organized collections for the African Missionaries, the poor of the parish and Bobby Calvary's operation. I helped rebuild MacLollard's fence the time it fell down. I've supported the Tennis Club Walkathon, the training of Guide Dogs for the Blind, better changing facilities for the rugby footballers and more frequent visits from the mobile library. I've written to the editor of the *Post* demanding guttering for Sandilands Place. I've raised my voice against the proposed sewerage scheme, the subdivision of Plymouth Hill, the timetable at the train station and the state of the underpass. But I've lost interest. I've reached the stage where, if I get a letter for the RSL, I have to look up the secretary's name.

What is more, three of the six victims had Welsh names. Now it's known I've never had much time for the Welsh, ever since they served me late leeks at a wedding breakfast once. Even Jack-in-the-ditch knows that. When you take these little things one at a time they seem inconsequential. But when you add them up, they make you wonder.

I think Arblaster was right when he said someone is trying to set me up. The questions are, who and why? I am a humble postman, as Sir William Gilbert might have written.

Now are the bees related to the implement? Have I any reason to believe that the falling of shutter 63 in such a way as to implicate me in a dastardly deed and to bring upon my head the wrath of Telecom and Australia Post, is other than coincidence? Not at present, but I think you take my point. Who says shutter 63 fell at all? Whose word is there but mine? I shot the cat, I killed the dog, why would I not murder the horses? There are quite a few people hereabouts who would see that as a crime worse than fighting prostitution. I've never been popular here, though I've done my bit.

Not for one moment do I believe anyone here is the Ripper. I *do* believe someone here knows what the implement is – after all, it was described, albeit inaccurately, in the *Bulletin* – and wants me out of town. It's not important I be charged, let alone convicted, of a crime. Mud sticks.

There's the stall ahead. We won't find Derry there, he hasn't been seen since World War II. He leaves the honey here in the stall and the buyer puts the price in the tea chest. People come from far and wide to buy this honey. I think it's the concept of a stall selling honey on the honour system that so appeals to them. Mind you, Derry won't take money, that's one thing he has no use for. He'll take clothing, tins of smoked salmon, bottles of Scotch and tobacco.

We'll take the smallest container here in exchange for this packet of pumpernickel I found in the back of the fridge. He has to spread his smoked salmon on something. I can't for the life of me see how an absconding swarm could be forseen. They leave no queen cells. Mind you, I've a lot to learn about bees.

I'm *sure* someone dug a hole and interfered with that telephone cable. Probably somewhere near Isbester's house, where it's still covered in clay. I thought it might have been the Balthazars, they're awake all night, but it could have been anyone. Every Dog Rock resident has at least one reason for wanting me gone. My head's spinning. I'll have to stop thinking about it. I'll think about my holidays instead.

They're right about this honey: this is honey made with a dash of sugar syrup. Now what in the *Hell* is going on, that Terry Derry should stoop to this?

5 I've kept very busy since we last met. Taking advantage of a decent night's sleep on Tuesday I got my spuds in Wednesday. You can imagine my satisfaction when it started to pour rain Wednesday night. I didn't go out of my yard all day Wednesday, except to clear the pokies that night. It's the men's midweek triples Wednesday, and Bert was still in the clubhouse at 9 p.m. I thought he might be, so I took the honey in for his missus. I still have a fair bit left from last season, candied now, but well flavoured. The snappygum flowered all over the state last February, creating a late flow. I was still extracting well into March.

'Ar blast her,' he says, 'she shouldn't have bothered you. Shouldn't have bothered your head! Terry Derry's honey is the best in the world, outside of Tasmanian leatherwood honey.'

'And have you tasted his last batch?' I inquired, as I cleared the Snow Goose and made for the Inca King.

'There's nothing wrong with it!' he says. 'Vince, you're not closing the bar yet?'

'Only you and D'Arcy here, Bert. And he'll be off to work in a minute.'

'But aren't I entitled . . .'

'Come on Bert,' says I. 'I'll bet he's been up here every night this week, eh Vince?'

'He never comes in Tuesday night, as he has to watch that *Dallas*. But he was here Monday, weren't you Bert?'

'I had to defend D'Arcy's reputation!'

It's a hard life, a dairyman's life. Up in the miserable darkness of dawn with the kookaburras, looking for cows in the mist. Bert had an Ayrshire herd, a beautiful herd to look upon. He supplied the milk to Dog Rock. He produced the milk and he supplied the milk, and the reason he built up an Ayrshire herd was to give the town the best milk he could. Ayrshires are rich creamers. Not as rich as Jerseys maybe, but as rich as Guernseys in this climate, and they'll keep grazing when the Channel Islanders are shivering in the trees with their arse to the wind. Then the Milk Board was set up to create work where none existed and to tell him his milk was a health hazard and to pay him the same for his rich Ayrshire milk as the Friesian producers get for their watery Friesian milk, and they can produce twice the volume. I suppose you know it's an offence to sell milk: did you know it's an offence to give it away?

There's no play on Monday, we give the greens a day of rest. Only the hard core come in Monday, and Bert, who never drank a drop of liquor or put a coin in a poker machine or held a bowl in his hand till he was sixty-five years of age, has been making up for lost time.

I hear he's been leading young ASM O'Toole astray recently.

I mentioned the fig in the aviary to him and he claimed it was his idea. Says he recommended it to the Balthazars as a means of making an income.

'Poor little buggers,' he says, as I usher him out the door. 'I remember the last Depression, D'Arcy. Unemployment's a dreadful thing. Those lads own nothing, it breaks my bloody heart. I said to them, have you seen the derelict orchards out Cow Flat? No one can make a living off them now. True, the fruit trees are still there, the roadside stalls are open, but they're owned by city people now and they're putting money in, not taking it out. They survive for five years on average, then they go broke and sell to someone else from the city, who survives another five years, and so it goes. Once those orchards were thriving concerns. What's the matter with the world, D'Arcy? They pay them now to pull the trees *out!*'

'The trees have to be sprayed continually, Bert. The drug companies charge what they can get for the sprays.'

'No doubt that's part of it, but the main trouble is *birds*. There are more birds today then there were yesterday. Unless you're prepared to roam your orchard night and day with a twenty-two, the birds eat half your crop. I said to the boys, if you could design a cheap, effective, efficient means of protecting fruit crops from birds, you mightn't make much out of it yourself, but you'd be boosting the economy. So they planted a fig tree in the aviary for starters. D'Arcy, what do we owe you for the honey?'

'I'll get it off you some time I don't have to take it in twenty-cent pieces. Now you're sure you'll be right to get home?'

'I'll take the short cut through Hathaways. Have you been to Venice, D'Arcy? That Lombard von Lumpsum was trying to tell Vince tonight Lucerne is better than Venice! Good Lord, I should know, I've been to them both.'

'Sweet dreams, Bert.'

'Sleep well, D'Arcy.'

But as it happened, I did not sleep well. I lay awake till midnight, brooding over where to put my bees and other matters, then at 3 a.m. in the middle of the bloody night, Vera Topwaite wanted International.

Thursday I shifted the bees. It was wet all day so they weren't foraging. I took them to Hardacre's at Barren Grounds. They'll do no good out there, but that's what people want for them. I'd as soon sell them as eat thistle honey.

Thursday night I had my weekly meeting with Jack-in-the-ditch. You know, in many ways, I'm sorry for Jack-in-the-ditch. He got off to a dreadful start here when he stopped Mrs Hardacre for speeding when she was racing to catch the train at Bonny Tops so little crippled Aggie could go on the school excursion. He wouldn't be forty and he's got a daughter eighteen who comes in at 2 a.m., and a daughter two who wakes up four hours later, and several sons in between. Natalie's always covered in kitten scratches and Jenny's got hickeys on her neck from love bites. I thought she had ringworms when I first met her.

It must be very hard making ends meet. He sells a lot of fox skins. Normally, a constable is lockup keeper, but here it's the sergeant's job. He's on call twenty-four hours a day. Where he came from, he could get the JPs to issue forty-eight hours' hard labour in the lockup, which meant chopping the copper's wood and digging his garden for him, but here, he has to do that himself. He can't keep anyone longer than overnight. Drunks are held and released on their own recognizance, if they can recognize themselves in the shaving mirror at first light. Young Wayne Mercaptan, Ethyl's son, spends more time in there than anyone else. I believe he keeps his own toothbrush in a rack in the left-hand cell. He's the man famous for calling at D'Oilycart's and asking for a tankful of juice, when he's just filled up at the Ampol down the road. Thirty cents' worth; maybe he's forgetful or maybe that's his idea of a joke. Anyway, he rolled his Torana last winter: just left it down the bank and limped home to bed. Cadwalloper saw it on patrol, went straight round to his house and dug him out, gave him the roadside alcotest. The biggest problem in this town, though, is kids riding bikes on the footpath.

'D'Arcy, come in mate. Sit yourself down. I'm just trying to work through these bloody bail forms they sent me. All I needed under the Summary Offences Act was an undertaking to appear in court. I never took more than a dollar but they showed up every time. Never had one fail to front on me. Now, there's a million bloody forms in a dozen languages and no money. Look at this! A 5A Bail Form in Turkish! Why don't they ask us coppers before they do this sort of thing? You know I can't interview a juvenile now except in the presence of his parent? Once, if I caught a kid riding on the footpath and wanted to give him a scare, I could bring him in here and leave the lockup door open. But who's he going to look at if Mum's sitting where you are? How can I keep them off the footpath now?'

'Sergeant, you'll be pleased to hear I've moved the bees. Can we look at the photo?'

'Be right with you, mate. You know that Izzard's golden Labrador walks round with its head in a plastic bucket to stop it licking its sores? Ever had a go at you on the bike?'

'Not to my recollection.'

'Didn't think so. Got a complaint here it was seen worrying some coloured sheep out Plymouth way, but I don't reckon it could worry much with a plastic bucket over its head. Times I feel I've got a plastic bucket over *my* head and a muzzle on as well.'

'Have you any clues as to the Ripper's identity, Sergeant?'

'Be right with you, D'Arce. Got to fill out this accident report. I'm sorry to hear you've decided not to play with me in the State Pairs.'

'I'm pretty sure to be playing cricket. It wouldn't be fair to you. You're a better player than me anyway.'

'I know how you must feel, D'Arce. But I have a job to do, same as you. This is a bloody accident never should have happened! You know that one-lane bridge the other side of Cow Flat? Well Alec Beaudesert was half way through varnishing his rumpus-room floor when he realized he'd made an error in his estimates. He was heading back from the hardware with half a litre of Estapol satin, when Winton Worrywart's old Jersey housecow come down with milk fever. *He* was heading off to the vet's to buy two packs of calcium gluconate. Neither one of the buggers would back off, just flashed their lights and blew the horn. Worst of it is, I've a complaint from the ambulance officer they were fighting in the back of the ambulance.'

'That Beaudesert's a handyman and a half. I hear he keeps a fuel stove burning on the stumps of his wire brushes. And didn't he once start painting the roof of a house in unsettled weather?'

'That'd be him. Of course, the rumpus room was ruined and the cow died. She was thirty-two years old, though, Winton milks 'em till he can't fit a bucket under. Now then, where's that photo?'

We placed the photo before us on the table and sat contemplating the implement.

'It occurs to me, D'Arcy, if you fitted *this* end to a bar counter, you could use this end to pull the cork from a jeroboam of champagne.'

'By the same token, if you fixed *this* end to the branch of a tree, Sergeant, you've a combination block and tackle for butchering wild pigs in the field. This'll be your detusker.'

'You don't detusk wild pigs! The usual thing's to leave them where they drop or cut the head off for a trophy. Tusks are good for nothing mate, and you can't eat them, they're full of worms.'

'In that case, why would you need a special decorker for champagne bottles? Standard practice is to shake the buggery out of them. And what's *this* supposed to be?'

'Well that could be for washing bottles. You could fix a bottlebrush to that. And *this* could be a can crusher and this is to hang your bar towel on.'

'You're just guessing.'

'I've been thinking about the whole business. You know what *I* reckon? I reckon someone in this town wants me transferred.'

'Bullshit. Don't be ridiculous.'

'I enforce the law, or rather, I try to see it's obeyed. I don't make too many friends doing that. I use my discretion and I don't take bribes, and that way, I wind up making enemies of everyone. I won't enforce a warrant on someone I think needs time to pay!'

'What are you raving on about?'

'I suppose it's coincidence three of those six victims had Welsh names and one was a sportsman? I have a Welsh name and I am a sportsman. I must look pretty stupid with a Ripper on my beat. The town must wonder why I'm so stupid. Why can't I come up with a suspect? And the longer it drags on the more stupid I look. I must be a dumb copper, mate. There are plenty of coppers with hobby farms. Ex-coppers, most of them. City coppers, all of them. Mark my words, there's plenty of locals keen to see the back of me.'

'This is madness! I won't listen to more.'

'Not for one moment do I believe anyone here is the Ripper. I *do* believe someone here knows what the implement is, and wants me out of town.'

'Now let's suppose, for the sake of argument, this fantasy of yours is correct. One of the 776 residents, perhaps the publican, goes to the PO to post a letter, sees or is shown the implement, and both knows what it is and recognizes it, from its description in the press, as the Ripper's murder weapon. Why does he, or she, not come forward with the information?'

'Because he, or indeed she, was the person who put it in the mail.'

'Then to whom was it addressed?'

'You know as well as I do, D'Arcy, it wasn't addressed to *any*one. One of the things that worries me is why you've kept this to yourself.'

'Kept what to myself?'

'If you hadn't murdered Jennings' cattledog, I might never have seen that wombat. But I knew the minute I smelt it, it had been dead for some days. So I did the rounds of the garages.'

'All right, before you go any further: if *you* knew that accident was rigged – and I knew as soon as I saw that implement Fargo would never have taken it out, it was far too heavy and bulky, he'd have carded it for sure.

Plus, it was on the right-hand side of the bike and he puts his OAs in the left-hand bag – why couldn't you take me into your confidence?'

'Because who better than you . . .'

'Is that right? And who better than *you*? A policeman who patrols the Cow Flat Road every day and night of his life!'

'You've never liked me, D'Oliveres. But why would you stoop to this?'

'You think you've pretty nicely set me up, don't you Cadwalloper. What's the word of a postal worker compared to that of a policeman? I expect I've you to thank for the falling of shutter 63.'

'I can't be goaded into assault by the likes of you.'

'In that case, you're an ignorant colonial! And I'll stay in this town till it suits me to get the sack.'

'Get out of here, you Pommy bastard! 'Fore I hang one on ya!'

I don't really think it was him about the shutter at all. He *is* a better player than me. But the fact he could not take me into his confidence over the wombat has made further collaboration between us impossible. The reason I didn't take him – or, for that matter, you – into *my* confidence, was I don't want Renee, Carmel & Co spreading these things round town. Oh well: I'm glad we're not playing pairs, though we still have to face each other on the House Committee.

Friday I rested and gave some thought to the propagation of rumour. When two or more gather together in Dog Rock, rumour is not just transmitted but modified, more in accordance with what should never have been, as distinct from what actually happened. A town's image of itself – its gossip – is the inverse of its tourist information, and serves the function of verbal grooming, subject to mobilization as censure. To confide in a second party one's disapproval of a third in no way prevents one from doing the same with the third in the absence of the second. On the contrary, it may *oblige* one, for the imbalance of rumour is a town's chief weapon of control. Outsiders are initially subjected to a period wherein they are the butt, but do not share in, slander. During this period their house will continue to be known as the house of the previous occupant. If and when the collective subconscious decides there is no getting rid of them, they may be told about Wayne Mercaptan's accident, or Barry Bitterbest's rudeness to the greengrocer. If, at this point, they clumsily fail or refuse to reciprocate with a titbit of their own, they run the risk of permanent rejection.

An inventive and productive flow of malicious gossip is a diagnostic sign of good health in a town, as it serves to bond the residents, convincing each one he has the goods on the others while they know nothing of him. In Dog Rock, an influx of newcomers too vast for the town to assimilate into its gossip networks has already produced pockets of the classical urban impasse, where everyone minds his own business and no one speaks to anyone. An ugly situation, but uglier by far is that seen in declining, moribund communities, which are populated by citizens as brutally frank as they are miserable. Where gossip is perverted into silence or honesty, community persists in name only.

I thought of tracking that rumour, but though I know where I'd finish up, I wouldn't know where to begin. I'd finish up at the PO, the exchange, the Bowling Club, the public bar of the Dog Rock hotel, the newsagency, the CWA hall or the C of E Ladies Guild. I can just hear someone like Vera Topwaite saying, to the clink of saucers being washed, 'Did you hear about the postman's bees?' Then someone like MacLollard, who's measuring up cupboards, chips in with his five penneth worth. 'I don't say D'Arcy did it, but if he did, good luck to him. I've had no time for horses since Amanda Calvary's pony ate my Phenomenal Earlies.' No, I've better things to do at the moment than track down vicious rumours. I want to break in this new pair of walking boots, for one thing.

Yesterday, being Saturday, I went down town for the papers early and spent the morning reading the prestige real-estate columns in the *Australian*. I always buy the

Australian. I used to buy the *National Times* as well, but it's gone off something dreadful lately. I don't know what they've done to it. When you stick the match down it seems to char, rather than burn, and what flames you do get hardly suffice to ignite the pine cones. I was looking at the Gold Coast, to tell you the truth. If the worst comes to the worst, I'll be glad to see the back of this place. But if it doesn't, there's no place on earth I'd rather live than here.

Yesterday arvo I went to the club, to tell them I might be playing cricket. Saturday night's the worst night on the exchange, as you can imagine. They'll stay up all night, some of them, and I try to get a few cans in and a bit of a snooze in front of the tube. As you see, I've the tele in the kitchen. When you're on your own, you live in your blessed kitchen. It's the warmest room in the house, because of the fuel stove. My hot water runs off the stove, that's what you can hear in the roof. It's boiling now. There's rats up there as well, but that's the stove. It's that efficient, my hot-water service, I have to bleed it, from time to time, by taking hot baths. I hate to see waste of any kind.

But it's a beautiful old stone house, and I do love colonial stone houses.

Saturday arvo we play men's fours. During the Pennants which is played in February – you're not going to wear those plimsolls, I hope! I wouldn't wear them, if I were you. No support for the ankle. You turn an ankle, I can't carry you! Very well then, as long as you understand.

Right then: tobacco, whisky, Mylanta, beer ... I don't think we'll need our jerseys. I don't believe in wet-weather gear. That wet-weather gear Australia Post issues reminds me of the skin on a tin of yellow plastic paint. I'm glad I don't ride a pushbike; the slightest exertion, and you're more wet on the inside than what you are on the out. No, what you want in wet weather is a rough, raw-wool jersey. It does you no harm to get soaked to the skin, provided you don't get cold.

I'm the skipper of the number three pennants team, and Mr Justice Safehouse is keen to play in my side. As it happens, I'm looking for a second, I want to get rid of Truelove. One copper a team is plenty, some might say too many. If I hear any more about the new Crimes Act, I might commit some sort of crime myself. And I don't want to take Arblaster from the lead until he's learned to let the *bowl* do the work. He's usually three feet short with his first bowl and six feet over with his second, but it's only his first season, and he's keen, you must give him that.

I can't see a judge talking to a copper, so I spent most of the afternoon with Dickie Safehouse. When I got home I watched *Countdown Flipside* and had a few more tinnies. I'm afraid to say they had to ring me to get me to come in at 10 p.m. It's the stress, you see.

What a night I had last night! I couldn't get to sleep till way past 3 a.m. It was like trying to get to sleep in a youth hostel full of French schoolboys. There were two parties last night. Brian O'Bastardbox had all the district trendies in, to celebrate his acquisition of a beautiful antique dairy cabinet that would have cost $5,000 if he'd bought it from an antique dealer. Foggy Hollow were round at Newcomers, to celebrate the sale, for one hundred bucks, of a piece of old junk furniture that's stood on Newcomer's verandah fifty years, because no one could be bothered carting it to the tip. O'Bastardbox seems depressed; it shows in his gum-tree paintings. He was renowned for his gay, frothy studies of ghost gums and scribbly barks; now, a deep gloom seems to have settled on him, and he favours gnarled, twisted little mallees on headlands, and swamp mahoganies. Here's hoping his bargain cheers him up: he's the toast of the town's ladies.

Then, just when I thought it was safe to put the light out, bloody Wayne Mercaptan is run off the road at the substation. He can't believe it's happened again, so he sits there, as though he's in Church. I think it must have been reported ten times, before I started saying, 'If it's about that accident, we know.' I see no reason to keep waking the poor copper's wife all night.

I say, I'm looking forward to this walk! The tension's building up in me. I don't think I've felt so uneasy since Bernie Dwyer drove me home from Bonny Tops in second gear the whole way, because he was too busy running down painters, dockers, storemen and packers to think what he was doing. I was hoping to see the Isbesters this weekend, but I believe they've gone skiing. Mal rang Bert from a restaurant Friday and said (in a loud voice), 'That cow calved yet?' 'No, she hasn't calved yet,' replied Bert, 'though she did calve a week ago.'

We'll leave the car at Arblaster's fire trail and strike out across country. I managed to get hold of some of Terry Derry's honey from last season and by Jove, it's dense: good bit of ti-tree in it. Not a trace of snappygum. It's believed Terry keeps his bees in the National Park, which is against the law, and I'd say, from the appearance and taste of the honey, he's got them near a wet heath. God knows why he's feeding them syrup, let alone selling the honey. I reckon we should make for the wet heath, just to give us a purpose. It's not like walking at home, here. You never know where you're headed.

One thing I've often wondered, is how Terry gets his honey out. He must have a mule or two. I'm worried about him, to tell you the truth, I'd worry about any bee man who fed his bees sugar. I don't think he moves his hives. One big bloodwood will give enough nectar to fill ten supers with honey. From what he sells, I don't think he'd have more than forty or fifty hives, and I reckon they'd be painted a sort of khaki colour, and covered in netting. I wonder if those were his bees that killed Miss Hathaway's horses. I've never known bees carry away their dead before. Perhaps he taught them to do it, he must have a lot of spare time.

If we leave the car here, Arblaster will see it, and since I wouldn't take his money the other night, he'll feel obliged to wander over with some meat, or a jar of cream. Nothing burdens a farmer's mind as much as a favour he hasn't repaid. If you want to be cruel to a farmer, do him a favour, then leave the country before he has the chance to repay it. He'll never sleep in peace again.

Bert won't see the car from here. We'll leave it behind this old man Banksia, then we'll head across this ridge, down into the gully then up the other side, then along the spur where the geebungs grow and back by the Dog Rock itself. If it's a clear, moonlit night, we might see a greater glider.

This is not my idea of walking country. I like to leave a village through a hedgerow, cross a field, pass by a farmer's barn, spend ten minutes in a wood, lunch in another village. If you didn't study Latin as a lad, you'd be hard pressed to memorize the names of these plants. No poet ever named them. Take that little thing there, for instance, Conesperma ericinum. Very common hereabouts, a mauve-flowering weed. 'Heath milkwort' is supposed to be its common name, most inappropriate, if I may say so. It should be called something like 'Wino's nosegay' to fix it in antipodean memories. I see signs of a self-defensive mysticism among the local Balthazars. If it's a crime to give a thing a name, you don't feel so bad about being ignorant. I'll guarantee the guru at the ashram can't tell one boronia from another.

It's the thought of the trip back home once a year that allows me to endure this place. What monotony! Frost this morning in the shadows of the trees like compass needles pointing north, New Holland honeyeaters in the heath-leafed Banksias, every year the same. Back home in the mist there'll be a nimbus round the streetlights, but no hansom cab outside my Mexican pines. Still, I mustn't complain. A month over there disillusions me more completely than forty-eight weeks here, and I'll tell you a funny thing: the only local I think of when I'm there, as distinct from write to, is Dion Belvedere. Yes, because Dion is the most naturally talented cricketer I have ever seen. When he can be bothered, he opens the batting for us. The rest of them wear cream flannel trousers: Dion and I wear white tennis shorts. He arrives on his motorcycle, always late, always hung-over. He ambles out, doesn't take strike, doesn't believe in taking strike. He looks at the field placings, shares a joke with the wicket keeper, shares a joke with the umpire (Goodfellow), taps his borrowed bat in the block-hole. Much of the time he's gone first ball, but if he survives that first over, a crowd begins to gather at the windows of the clubhouse. If I'm at the other end of the wicket, half the time I forget to run, I'm that mesmer-ized. I have never known a batsman demolish an attack as early in the innings as Dion. There is not a trace of caution in his make-up. He will cut a ball off his leg stump. He will square drive a yorker. He has no more respect for a good length delivery than he has for an inswinging bouncer. He has not a single defensive stroke in his entire repertoire. He can hit any ball bowled to him to anywhere on the field, off the middle of the bat.

Now to me, and I think to most men, there is nothing more demoralizing than this kind of natural sporting ability in a man who doesn't value it. I wish I had it. If I did, I'd be playing for England. Dion was selected in the dis-trict side to play the Pakistanis a few years back: he didn't turn up. He preferred to take his girlfriend pillion to the city on the day instead. When I rebuked him for his lack of ambition – a thing I find hard to forgive in any man – he replied there were more important things than cricket, which, when all's said and done, is just a stupid game. At this, a great cheer went up from the very ordinary talents drinking with him, and I began to understand, for the first time perhaps, the nature of the Dog Rock hero. I have thought about it a good deal since and it worries me as much as it fascinates me. In some mysterious way, Dion's failure to amount to anything *magnifies* us. It's the sort of secular religious truth that cries out for a maypole and a Morris dance. One of these days he's going to come off that bike and break his back in five places. I wonder if he'll watch the cricket from his wheelchair, and if so, what he will think of it.

Let's stop here a minute, by the yellow pea flowers and the Ledum boronia. Phew, I'm puffed. Smoke too much when you're on the exchange. Care for a swig?

What, don't drink Mylanta? I might have a whisky, just the one sip. Big mail tomorrow, bound to be. Monday's always a big mail. Don't think the *Geographic*s have arrived yet. Haven't got mine, anyway. I wouldn't like a kick in the pants for every *Geographic* in this town.

By George, I'm looking forward to walking that Cotswold Way! I hope they haven't had too much rain, it gets rather muddy in wet weather. I'll leave the old Chipping Camden market hall, and I'll wander down to Broadway by the Kiftsgate Stone, and on the way I'll have a pint of mild at the Fish Inn. I won't stop in Broadway, it's full of Americans. I'll head up towards Snowshill, by the county boundary through the kissing gate.

What is it I miss most, you ask? That's easy. The woolstaplers' halls, the coaching inns, the medieval crosses and the churches.

Oh dear, I'm supposed to be in Church! Never mind, I'll go to evensong.

Our English settlers did what they could out here, but they couldn't reproduce it completely. On the credit side, we enjoy the parrots and fewer American tourists. I quite like the blending of the softwoods and hardwoods here, the natives in among the liquidambars, claret ash, golden elm, Monterey pine – Scotland's covered in sycamores and rhodos. You take the house names here. Half the houses don't have a number. It's a relief postman's nightmare, this place. You should see the mail I get addressed to 'Mrs Calvary, Dog Rock'. You've got to be a bit of a detective in this game. You've got to be a bit shrewd. God help you if it goes to the wrong Mrs Calvary. Some of them don't speak to the others.

We've a Nirvana and a Shangri-la, a Woodlands and a Bonny View. We've a Greenfields, a Green Meadows, a Spring View, a Spring Hill, a Green Bank, a Springfield and a Spring Vale. We've a Lost Croft, a Fern Lodge, a Greentrees, a Strayleaves, a Silvertrees, a Greenslopes, a Sunnybank and a Sunnybrae. We've a Holly Cottage and a Holly Lodge. We've a Greenacre View, a Grinton Lodge, a Barnard Castle, a Rosewood, a Red Gums, a Dal Lake and a Grasmere. We've a Pinewood, a

Piney Vista, a Pinehaven, a Pine Cottage, a Pine Hill, a Piney Ridge, a Pineview and a Pine Lodge. We've an Inverness, an Aberdeen, a Firth of Forth, a Killmarnock, a Pen Glen, an Innes Bryn and a Ferniehirst. We've a Dover, a Windsor, a Palmerston, a Doddington, an Epping, an Eastwood, a Concord and a Lincoln, but also a Yabbydah, a Warrigal, Kwinana, Belambah, Coolgardie, Wahroongah, Taronga, Linga Longa . . . I could linger longer, but I've made my point: there's something *missing* here. And what's missing here, is over there. But what's missing over there, is here.

Winchcombe was the capital of the Kingdom of Mercia and I have Mercian blood on my mother's side: I guess that's it, in a nutshell. It takes centuries to acclimatize. I dare say my Anglo-Saxon ancestors were most uncomfortable in Mercia, to begin with. And by the time those Humblebee cottages were built, on the hill by the Wadsfield Roman Villa – the Wadsfield Roman Villa! – the Normans had appropriated the land.

I'll spend the night in the Belas Knap long barrow. Sshh – over there. A man, see? Near that big turpentine. It's Balthazar Whitefriar, wearing no shoes. He's often down here, he's trying to come to terms with the place. He writes poems about his 'totem' bird. I wish him the best of British luck.

Don't feel like going on a walk now, can't stop thinking of the Humblebee cottages. Just want to sit here and drink this whisky. Tireder than I thought I was, you should never have let me open the bottle! I intend to empty it now.

Let's go over the whole business. There *was* an address on the implement, or why go to the trouble of finding a dead wombat by the side of the Cow Flat Road? No, the cattle-dog chewed it off. I'd say it was addressed to me. Fargo delivers *my* heavy parcels. I'm the only customer so favoured. Jack-in-the-ditch picks his mail up at the counter. What's the idea in it? Simple. Use the town's gossip networks to discredit me, an outsider. Why, I can't imagine. I've done my bit. Horses poisoned, blue in the face. Anginine. Saw it as soon as I walked in the stables.

Had to pretend to go along with things. Taking you into my confidence now, must be the whisky talking. Never drink in the public bar for that very reason. Know too much! Mrs Calvary, Dog Rock, I ask you. If they want to go out, they ring the exchange. 'Oh Carmel, I'm just going across to my sister's place for a few minutes, so if Dougie calls, would you put him through – now, wait a minute: I have to go to the butcher's first, that's right. And then, the school will be out, so tell him to ring back at four, if you wouldn't mind.'

They'll miss that exchange. It's nothing but a bloody answering service.

Can hardly keep my eyes open. Would you mind if I shut them a minute?

What's the time? *Five o'clock!* You should have woken me. Now we've just time for a peek at the plurry Dog Rock before we go back. It's always a good night for the Beeb on channel 2, Sunday night.

I'll get the force onto Derry, let the Sergeant do the footwork. I'm flying out of here Monday the first of October, two weeks from tomorrow. I never needed a holiday so badly in my entire life!

6 What a night and day and night I've had, if you include seeing Balthazar Whitefriar talking to the Dog Rock Sunday night, under the stars, the way we did. It wasn't so much him talking to it as it talking back, that worried me. What do you suppose it meant when it said, 'If you would know my majesty, son, fly on green wings in the dead of night'? I thought I recognized the voice, though, despite the Aboriginal accent. I found a little cassette there once. Got it at home, but can't play it on the Stromberg-Carlson.

Anyway, I've had no time to think about it since. Everything went wrong for me yesterday. I couldn't find the flag, it was in the drying room. Then the mail train was late. The *National Geographic*s were on it when it came. Mail count day yesterday: every item for dispatch and delivery and redirection to be counted.

There were two mail bundles for Tennant Creek in our bags. We get a lot of mail for Tennant Creek here, why, I couldn't tell you. Mail! You never saw such a heap of unsolicited rubbish in all your life. Free offers from the *Reader's Digest* by the bloody armload. *Australia Post Stamp Collector Bulletin*s, forty-seven of them. Too big to fit in any box on the beat, but marked, 'Not to be folded'. How can they do it to us? Bags everywhere: he never inverts them and he never sends them back, he's a hoarder of empty mail bags. Then that bastard from the Funny Farm, in at five past nine, wanting to know when the sorting would be done. They must think I can't hear. I said to the PM, you can tell him to come back at 10.15 a.m.

I couldn't get the blessed bike to start. It should have gone in for a service last week, but he never took it up. He's dropped it again, there are four fresh sandstone-coloured scratches on the left-hand rear-vision mirror: front fence of the Ghostloaf Grange again, I'll guarantee. And if *he* won't check the battery water, where's the point me doing it? But I had three letters for him in the mail and one for myself; that's typical.

Mine was of the windowed variety, on which the address becomes progressively fainter as the colour turns from white to blue then pink.

I was in a pretty bad mood before the rain even started. Rain! Sleet! I've known nothing like it. It got inside my singlet. I said to the PM, if anyone complains about wet mail today, watch out. You can't look ahead of you in sleet like that. You have to look sideways or your eyes get cut. By the end of plug one my hands were so cold I couldn't untie my bundles. I *know* I had a parcel of film for Jack Mouth, but when I looked for it, it was gone.

Then, when I went home at lunchtime, as I'd feared, the rain had washed away my onion seedlings.

The mail here closes at 3 p.m. and leaves on the 3.30 train. At 20 to 3 an urgent telegram arrived for Dodgecastle, so I took it straight round. At 5 to 3, Mrs Nightingale came in with 375 bereavement thank you cards. Does the PM say, leave them till tomorrow D'Arcy, they're not urgent? No, he wants them in the count, for the same reason he forces every kid he meets to subscribe to the *Australia Post Stamp Collector*.

So I went on regulation strike and missed the train, to make a point. There were two priority paid letters in the mail and they're going to be late, but I don't care. I went straight round to see Fargo after knocking off, and I said to him, would you have done as I did?

'I'd have done just as you did,' he replied.

It's nothing to do with Mrs Nightingale, though she could have shown more consideration. I feel sorry for that woman. Between you and me, she's the one who waits by the box. The circumstances surrounding her late husband's death were frightening and tragic. He told her he had business in Mt Gambier, and was killed in a traffic accident in Townsville. They were supposed to be the happiest couple in town too, it makes me glad I'm single. No little painted glamour puss will ever do that to me.

Sambo was no doubt pleased with my performance, but after last night, what price would *he* be? The PM called him in this morning, read us both the Riot Act. Spoke to us the way he claims he's going to speak to the customers the day before he retires. Reckons he talked to the District Manager, but Carmel knows nothing of it. Only a jumped-up counter-jumper anyway. Never been so disappointed in a pair of postal workers. The scandal of the district. Socks to be pulled up and garters to be worn.

I heard the whistle blow of course, there wouldn't be anyone didn't. Must have woken the whole town. My hot water bottle was still warm, so I'd been in bed not more than two hours. I'd put the time at round midnight. You can't hear the late alarm from here, but I did hear something I think important, that no one else has mentioned; about 10 past 12 a semitrailer started up somewhere in the town. I mention this only because, today on the run, I noticed a large flock of galahs feeding on the railway track near the underpass.

Today being Tuesday, the mail was light, I had a bit of time on my hands. Here then, is my reconstruction of the events of last night, Monday September 17th.

At or about 10 p.m., APO Sambo Fargo and his bull terrier Banjo report for duty at the Dog Rock telephone exchange, dripping wet. It's a cold, misty night outside and quiet in the exchange. Banjo at once falls asleep by the radiator, while Fargo rereads the *Big Up Front Swinger* magazine he found at the tip. The night alarm cuts in at 10.30 p.m. and Fargo tests it once before retiring, failing to note if Banjo stirs, but as he says himself, the dog's no fool: he would open one eye, see Fargo was awake, go straight back to sleep.

ASM Bobby Calvary is on duty at the Dog Rock railway station. ASM Nigel de Rego is on duty at the Barren Grounds railway station. ASM Wayne Mercaptan, who has been on duty since 3 p.m. at the Plymouth railway station and who is very much looking forward to getting to bed tonight as he's had no sleep since late Saturday, has just found out he has to work a double shift, as ASM O'Toole has not reported for work and SM grade 4 Addiboy is on too high a rate of pay to relieve an ASM. If a chain is as strong as its weakest link, the State Rail Main Western Line is now as strong as Wayne Mercaptan, who can hardly hold his eyelids open, and is jogging up and down the signal-box steps, between gulping cups of instant coffee.

ASM Bobby Calvary has had to shunt an eighty-truck freight train, too long for the down refuge siding, onto the up line, to let the Flier through, and is noting final details in the signal-box register, when the Dog Rock up receive instrument brass bell rings, at 11.14 p.m., in a telegraph dating from the days of steam, once, then twice, then after a break once more, indicating that the Barren Grounds signalman (ASM de Rego) has received a signal from the King's Lynn signalman that a goods train is leaving King's Lynn for Barren Grounds. ASM Calvary acknowledges the signal, by plunging the brass commentator, and alters the up receive instrument from 'line closed' to 'line clear', making the appropriate entries in the register; time requested and time acknowledged, signal box in rear.

At 11.35 p.m. the Dog Rock up receive instrument bell rings again, as the train leaves Barren Grounds. ASM de Rego alters his dispatch instrument to 'train on line', automatically switching the Dog Rock receive instrument from 'line clear' to 'train on line', and ASM Calvary plunges his up dispatch commentator to alert the Plymouth signalman, ASM Mercaptan, that a train is entering the section Barren Grounds to Dog Rock. He notes in the register time departure received signal box in rear, and time requested signal box in advance, but he cannot enter time acknowledged signal box in advance, as Wayne Mercaptan is sound asleep, unable to acknowledge anything. The Plymouth up receive instrument is still in the 'line closed' position.

ASM Calvary now takes the handcloth from the signal frame, and, with one foot on the frame, pulls mightily to reverse, in smart succession, signal levers 20, 21, 23 and 24. As he does so, the lower light on the up signal near Sandilands Place, which being a fishtail distant signal, has a fixed upper green light, changes from red to green, but the light on the up signal near the swimming pool doesn't change from red, because this signal, being a starting signal, is overruled from the signal box in advance; no train can enter the section Dog Rock to Plymouth, until the Plymouth signalman alters his up receive instrument from 'line closed' to 'line clear'.

Realizing Mercaptan has gone to sleep, a not uncommon occurrence, Bobby Calvary pounds away on the dispatch commentator, trying to wake the man. One bell now, for speak on phone. Calvary can hear the train approaching, from the cutting near the Cow Flat quarry. He picks up the signals phone, gives one long and two short revolutions of the handle for Plymouth. No answer. The train goes through: the up home signal and the up second home are in the clear, but the starting signal isn't: no doubt swearing, the engineman applies the brakes, disturbing the hotel fornicating couples. Ten-dollar fine for Mercaptan now: traffic control in the city must be advised as to why the train stopped. It's a big wheat train, and Calvary is thankful the guard has a long walk to the signal box.

De Rego is on the blower now, wanting to know why the train's still in the section: another has left King's Lynn.

'Bloody Wayne's asleep, mate. Can't raise the bastard.'

'Ring him over the town phone.'

'Good idea. Oh, here comes the driver . . .'

It's Irving Calvary, with all the aplomb of the master of a small vessel.

'What's going on around here? Who's asleep?'

'Just trying to raise him now, Irv.'

'Mercaptan again. *I'*ll raise the bastard, I'll raise the bloody dead.'

In walks the guard. The observer's reading a paper.

'Ar, what's the matter, boys? Why we stopped here for?'

'Plymouth signalman's gone to sleep. Ring young Cliff at the general store to go over and wake him, why doncha, Bobby?'

'Can't raise Sambo, Irv.'

'*What!* Wait a minute, listen: don't I hear the late alarm? What's going *on* in this bloody town? *I*'ll wake the bastards, you watch me . . .'

'Please, Irv, no! Think of the children!'

'Ar, you better go and dig the copper out, mate. Get him to wake the operator.'

'Can't. Can't leave the station. Thirty-five-dollar fine.'

'Ar, all right, *I*'ll get him. Which way to the cop shop?'

I'm sure the late alarm woke the Sergeant, you can hear it plainly from the residence. And if it didn't, then the whistle would have; it woke every living creature within five miles, except Wayne, Sambo Fargo and Sambo's bull terrier. When the Sergeant found Wayne, after driving over to Plymouth in his dressing gown with the siren on –

he saw his daughter's boyfriend's car parked up a lane on the way – it took nearly ten minutes to wake him.

Irving was quite within his rights to blow the whistle, it's worked before with Wayne. The sound of a distant train whistle blowing non-stop is more likely to wake a sleeping ASM than the ringing of a nearby phone. Thirty-five minutes that train was delayed. There's a good chance Wayne will be demoted over it, and I wouldn't care to be Banjo, he's on starvation rations. When they finally broke down the exchange door, he woke and attacked the PM. Fargo locks it from the inside and leaves the key in the lock.

Coincidence? I'm on my way to see the Sergeant right now.

'Sergeant, I'd like to know what action you're taking over the events of last night.'

'What do you mean, you Pommy ratbag? Mercaptan falling asleep is a matter for the District Traffic Super-intendent. He wasn't drunk. Fargo falling asleep is a matter for the PM. Anyway, I hear he give yers *both* a good dressing down this morning.'

'So you regard two simultaneous defections of duty as coincidence. It's time you put aside racial prejudice and asked yourself a few hard questions. Have you done a swab on Fargo's dog? That's the first thing you should have done.'

'Geez, you Poms are animal obsessed. All you can think about is bees and horses and dogs and wombats.'

'And what have you done about Terry Derry?'

'I've got my hands full here. Something you, in com-mon with the rest of this town, don't seem to appreciate. I haven't time to go bashing through the bush looking for a man who's been missing forty years. Get the ranger onto it.'

'What would you say if I were to tell you, that just after you left the station last night on your way to Ply-mouth, a semitrailer started up somewhere in this town? The events of last night, together with the inferior quality of Derry's recent honey and that implement in the mail, add up to a major conspiracy.'

'By the way, we've caught the Ripper.'

'Eh?'

'That's right. Caught him Friday. Council worker from Innaloo. Fingerprints on the first victim's car.'

'But the first victim wasn't *killed* by the Ripper!'

'Personally, I'm glad the matter's resolved. For your sake. You're a bit of a dark horse.'

'What do you mean?'

'It's not every postman can afford a trip to Britain every year. It's not every postman gets a whole heap of important-looking mail from Britain.'

'I see. So Fargo's been showing you my correspondence. You've been opening my mail.'

'I didn't open it. Didn't have to. But I *am* expecting the results of some inquiries into your background. You didn't fit in, D'Arce, never added up. Bringing out that Jowett Javelin was a mistake. I checked the rego.'

'You would.'

'You didn't buy that vehicle in Australia. It was imported from New Zealand.'

'So? The best flat four ever built.'

'There's something in your past you're keen to hide, D'Arce. Rest assured I'll find it. It was after you said you wouldn't play pairs with me anymore I decided to act.'

'You're bluffing.'

'You're shaking, D'Arcy. You've gone white as a sheet. You've a great sense of moral outrage, but you don't like policemen. That's a combination, over the years, I've learned to associate with criminals.'

'You've nothing on me, Cadwalloper. I'm a humble postman.'

'No, D'Arcy. You were shaking back there, mate, you went white. I'm *going* to make inquiries *now!*'

'Cadwalloper: as a fellow House Committeeman, may I ask a favour? Please don't inquire into my background. I've done nothing to be ashamed of.'

'Skeleton in the cupboard, eh D'Arce? Embryo in the bottle. I'll find it.'

'Let me say only this: I couldn't live the life of an ordinary postman back home. Despite what you colonials think, we don't all have money and we don't all own land. All I have is that Jowett Javelin, plus what I saved from my wages as a postman. Someone has sprung me, and set me up. Why? I've done my bit.'

'Come on, D'Arcy, it's now or later. Make it easy on yourself, make it now. I assure you, it will go no further.'

'Very well, I can see I have no choice. Do you mind if I smoke a cigarette?'

'Get on with it!'

'Very well. My father was the fourteenth Baron D'Oliveres, a well-known Cotswold fox-hunting man.'

'So. You're illegitimate.'

'I am not, oh what's the use, you may as well hear it, I am the fifteenth Baron, or rather, *was*, till I renounced the title.'

'*Renounced* a *title!*'

'I was working as the postman at Bourton-on-the-Water, and I found it adversely affecting . . .'

'D'Arcy: you get that title *back!*'

'Right, you've got the dirt on me, now let's get to work. I will take a sterile milk bottle . . .'

'Natalie! Sam! Hey, wait a bit: you wouldn't *bullshit* me, would you, D'Arce?'

'Well of course I would, and what's so frightening, is how very easily it's done.'

I am *still* the fifteenth Baron, but it's something I'd just as soon wasn't generally known here. They'll start asking questions like, why does a nobleman need a job? Why is he putting some poor, local unemployed person out of work, the rotten, stuck-up Pommy mongrel? Never mind that I inherited £500 worth of debts. I dare say my days at the PO are numbered. Cadwalloper caught me a bit off guard, oh well, I'll turn it to my own advantage. I can tough it out and they can't sack me. I'm a member of the Australian Postal Worker's Union (APWU).

But if we're to get to the bottom of this mystery now, we'll have to move fast. Whose truck was it? That's the first question. It must be one of three. We can ignore

Ben Chuckyfried, as he's a member of the National Party, and no member of the National Party would involve himself in anything dishonest. That leaves Wallace Worrywart and Hiram Hamburger. It's not just a question of tea-leafing wheat (and I dare say the Railways wouldn't miss a semiload): someone's in league here with our local villain to stock and supply Derry's stall. I wonder why he wants wheat? Of course, the incidents could be unrelated, but somehow, I don't think so. I'll ask FitzGibbon to swab Banjo, he keeps greyhounds; in fact, he owns a bitch by Undaunted, started but untried. And we'll find out why ASM O'Toole didn't report for work last night.

I think Hiram could be our man. He went and bought that Louisville rig the week before he lost his contract with the limestone works. His wife's been in Church a lot lately. And I overheard his neighbour, Alf Newcomer, at the club, saying how he often comes in at 3 a.m. and is gone again by 6. If logbooks weren't such a pack of lies we could ask the Sergeant to check his logbook.

I might go up and do the pokies now, and find out what Vince has to say. He hears a lot. He'll be closing early tonight too, *Dallas* night.

You never saw a happier man than Hiram when he bought that rig. He came here as storeman at the tractor factory (Co-op), and quickly realizing the need for a more efficient coast-to-highlands freight service, resigned and bought a truck that only half the big wheelers on the highway would wave at. I think this must have hurt him, and I suspect it sowed the seed in his mind that he would one day own his own semi, if it bankrupted him, which it will do. He was up and down that frightful pass, King's Lynn to the coast, six days a week. Built up quite a steady trade, but what a life. Five a.m. to 7 p.m. for half the pay of an ASM, and when he got home, he had to do the books. He'd have up to a hundred dockets in the cab, smeared with shredded lettuce from the Greasy Spoon. He began putting on weight as the business and worries expanded. It's a wise move, a precautionary move. Bert was remarking to me just the other day, how size is so important in the business world. Those big men can cope with the long lunches that drive their smaller opponents to the wall of the urinal. He was speaking of Isbester, but when you think of it, how many small, successful, middle-aged men do you see in this country? I went to a restaurant near Parliament House in Canberra once, my goodness: it looked like a Sumo wrestler's training camp, but a lot of important business was being done.

Sunday was oil and grease day; stuffing himself with French fries and chicken wings, Hiram would do a service on the truck. No time off for the self-employed. Sick as a dog, he drove still. He couldn't afford worker's comp insurance and couldn't trust a casual to take his one and only truck down the pass. That second hairpin is a shocker. Something ought to be done about it. If you're in a semi and you take the wrong line through the second hairpin – you've got to come right over to the wrong side of the road till you're scratching your right-hand mirror on the cliff face – one of three things happens, depending on how fast you're going: you go over the edge, you lay it on its side, or you get stuck in the middle. It's the young cocky's sons with their semi-loads of hay from up north that worry me: they often stop me on the run and ask which way to the pass. Seventeen years old they look, some of them, and the hay goes up seventy feet in the air. They're off before you can warn them of the second hairpin. No CB, so the other truckies can't warn them. They've been mulching the red cedar on that scarp with their blood and hay for years. I often wonder how they feel when they realize they're not going to make the second hairpin. Even Ben Chuckyfried, and he's an old hand, he got himself in a pickle there last year. Reckoned some hobby farmer come up round the second hairpin the way Dion does it on a motor cycle, forcing him to veer left. He knew he'd never make it; he felt the load shift, that horrible feeling you get when a tractor's going to roll. Couldn't reverse without jackknifing, so he parked it there, with the keys in the ignition, and walked back up to the boozer at the top of the pass to think. Blocked the pass for six hours, till the heavy crane arrived. Coppers tried to book him, but he blamed the whole thing on the Nominal Defendant. He's the bloke in the black Chevy Corvette who's always running Wayne Mercaptan off the road.

'Ar there, Vince.'

'You're a sly dog, squire. Play your hand pretty close to your gardening shirt.'

'Vince, I'll say this once, I've been a postman since I was forced to leave school early.'

'Tax worries, eh squire? I knew a bookie clocked on and off at Outwards Parcels for the same reason.'

'Don't drive me out, Vince. Don't lose this town a good postman.'

'No worries, squire. You're president next year. It's been resolved no one else will stand.'

'Hey! Who authorized this chook raffle you've got up here on the noticeboard?'

'Alf Newcomer.'

'But I barred him, he's supposed to be *barred.*'

'Give a battler a break, squire.'

'Will you stop calling me squire? A squire is a landed rural commoner. I am a landless rural postal worker. Where did Alf get the chooks to raffle?'

'Keep it quiet, they died of shock. Fox.'

'Last night, eh? By George, I wonder . . .'

This could be a stroke of luck for us. Hamburger's neighbour up half the night plucking chooks, you have to do it while they're still warm. I bet it was the fox that lives at the back of the service station in the bracken fern. I've seen him sunning himself by Dirk D'Oilycart's hoist in broad daylight.

I make it twenty minutes to *Dallas*, so we'll have to go straight round. Effectively, this next weekend will be my last for some time, so I must spend it hunting Derry. There's only three swamps within two miles of Hathaways on the map, if that's any indication. Two years ago we had a bad drought here and the coastal bloodwoods failed. Flowered, but the bees weren't interested. It's quite possible Derry could have moved his bees closer to town at that time.

Here we are then, Foggy Hollow. Bad-smelling place after rain. Nowhere the septic can seep away. The sewerage scheme will be forced on us soon because of Foggy Hollow, and it's the end of more than bad smells when people start thinking their shit doesn't stink.

There's Alf, shutting the door of his caravan. I wonder why he was out there. Three years ago he took his missus on a holiday to Sunraysia, where the fruit was so cheap she made that much jam he burnt the clutch out on his ute coming home. I like caravans, I lived in the caravan park here for years in an overnight van. They're the ones that look, from the knoll on Ninkum Street, like an out-apiary.

'Well, if it's not 'is Lordship! What an honour for this 'umble abode.'

God help us, it's Alf's son from next door, the rugby league footballer. I've heard he's a bit of a slipper man and a king-hit artist to boot. Three sheets to the wind, he's been into his clever kick. Poor Janine.

'D'yhear what I said t'ya?'

'I want to speak to your dad a minute, Tiger. You're blocking my way.'

Only boy in the whole Newcomer clan, this lad. Spoilt rotten. Always stopped off at the Zinnia on his way to the school bus. Bedroom to himself, with colour television. Own subscription to *Truck and Bus*.

'Too bloody right I'm blockin' your way! Nice, isn't it, when a Lord Muck like you can come out here and get a job. What about the unemployed?'

'You don't seem too badly off. Got a brand new car and a project home and a cabin cruiser.'

'My father struggled all his life for what I've got and he'll never own it. *I* had no advantages.'

'Come on now, you went to the best Catholic school in Bonny Tops!'

'Yeah? Only because me old man scrimped and saved to *send* me there. And where'd it get him? All I could land was a job up the yard.'

'Be fair, you'd be making boilers today if you'd finished your apprenticeship. And a yardman is on twice the pay of

118

any postal worker. When *I* was a lad I slept with a bunch of thieves and buggers in a cold wooden dorm. *I* had no loop-pile acrylic tufted carpet or Wellington cabinet in western walnut woodgrain. I was slaving night and day when I wasn't being thrashed or bastardized.'

It *is* a terrible place, Eton. I said to Tony Benn once, we could turn it into an orphanage for delinquents without changing a great deal.

'I don't think my old man wants to talk to you anyway. Takes it pretty hard when he's barred from his club by foreigners.'

'It doesn't stop him going there, though. He was there all last night with Hiram.'

'Hiram never goes *up* the club, so that's all you know, you dill! Where's you ermine stole?'

'I beg your pardon: Hiram left his truck parked at the club all night.'

'Bullshit! He drove off to a job while we was plucking the chooks.'

'Ah yes, but that's only because he was leaving on his interstate run!'

'Bullshit he was! He was back before we even got to the rooster!'

'You should have done the rooster first.'

'Get out of here, D'Arcy, 'fore I give you a kick for every Aussie working man you've put out of a job.'

So it *was* Hiram: we could confront him, but it won't do us any good, with the town against us. Ten to *Dallas*, I make it. FitzGibbon lives just round the corner, we'll see how he got on. I hear he can nose out twenty different foreign substances from one sniff of dog's urine.

'Simeon! How'd it go, mate?'

'I have to report the results of my inquiry have been communicated to the PM. I have no further comment to add at this stage, pending further investigation.'

I see: so that's the way the wind blows.

I hate this town so much at times I could knock ten years' growth off every blue spruce in the place with a pair of blunt nail clippers. They're Colorado blue spruce owners. If and when they sell the house – and who'd buy it – they put a clause in the contract excluding the blue spruce from sale. A blue spruce is never too big to transplant. Bruce the Goose's blue spruce was the biggest blue spruce I ever saw, and it was only fifteen feet high. He took it with him on his brick truck when he shot through with Leftwich's missus, its rootball in a big hessian sack. When I see a blue spruce in a front yard – and one was never planted in a backyard yet – I have a vision of a rust-coloured, rose linen, lumber-support rocker, still protected by the plastic in which it was delivered, swinging to the rhythm of a Custom Credit tennis tournament, while next to a buttoned, brown MacGregor tartan three-piece settee smelling of semen, on which a pouting schoolgirl, wearing a tooth brace, is painting her filthy nails with one eye on an early mass-produced clock, freshly painted in Estapol antique and fitted with an electric motor, a louring midget emerges from a corduroy beanbag, and flinging a child's high chair, in torn vinyl mustang, with cereals set on the beadings, at the Lladro stallion in the hutch of a colonial walnut china cabinet, hoarsely demands more crisps, an aluminium cricket bat, a BMX bike, a new watch-game, and a can of Fanta with a Big Mac, while Mother in the kitchen dies of shame as the fridge is moved to make way for the dishwasher. If it's war they want, they'll get war. I'll expose them for what they are, in the House of Lords. The only reason I retain the title, I like a say in the legislature.

All right, we'll go and visit ASM O'Toole at Plymouth railway station. He's one man who won't be watching *Dallas*. Nice situation when a postman has to do the unpaid work of a detective sergeant. Even *I* wanted to see what JR would have to say about Sue Ellen's, never mind. I'll find out tomorrow.

What? You're wondering why I never bothered to speak to Balthazar Whitefriar? (a) Because I conclude that whoever concealed that ghetto blaster in the Dog Rock is using the lad to reconnoitre the National Park and I believe I know why (question: what manner of creature in this park eats wheat? Answer: most of them); (b) because it's impossible to get any sense from him and always has been. He learned to control the weather on his last trip to India, though so far he hasn't willed it to do anything out of the ordinary. I admit I was puzzled at first, but those green wings in the dead of night are clear to me now, and the wheat theft has clinched it. Every second train is a wheat train these nights, easy enough to get one to stop for half an hour and load up at the underpass. The underpass can't be seen from any house, and the whistle served as a diversion.

Good heavens, is that a siren? What speed are we doing, hit the handbrake. Hello, he's got Nordette with him.

'I'd like you to return to the station, D'Arcy, and answer a few questions for me, please.'

'There was no need for the siren, Sergeant. And don't you think it might be a better idea to question ASM O'Toole? Hello Miss Pruvagol.'

'Good evening, D'Arcy, or should I say, me lord.'

'Banjo's urine has been tested, D'Arcy. Full of Serepax, mate.'

'Serepax! And would that do the trick eh, Miss Pru-vagol?'

'Knock it off, D'Arce, we know it was you, we just can't prove it, that's all.'

'Now wait a minute; I'm sure I'm not the only person in Dog Rock on Serepax.'

'That's for bloody sure, but you *are* the only person with a motive for discrediting Fargo!'

'Come off it, mate, *I* was the one suggested swabbing that dog in the first place!'

'Yes, you're a bit of a smart arse, D'Arce, but you might have come unstuck this time.'

'You astound me. And with a major series of crimes and conspiracies on your very doorstep.'

'You're the only criminal in this town. The Ripper made a confession. I've a copy of his deposition back at the station if you want to read it. Somehow, you got hold of that implement and you tried to use it to discredit Fargo, and when that backfired, you come up with some fanciful tale of shutters dropping, and when that didn't work you invented some cock-and-bull story about being

121

a baron, and then you poisoned a poor old dog. How low can a man get?'

'Are you laying formal charges?'

'No mate, you're too smart for that. But you'd better make some alternative arrangements, because your job will be going soon, and I don't advise you to stay on here. We've nothing against Pommies in Dog Rock, but we don't want the likes of you. And if you so much as attempt to interfere with another animal . . .'

'You mug! Can't you see this is *just* as she intended? I'm the only person hereabouts who could possibly spring her, and you want me out. You're playing into her hands.'

'What are you raving on about?'

'You're the last person I'd tell. I'm not completely certain so I'll keep nip till I am. The Ripper, I suppose, among other things. I'm taking sick leave, as of tonight. My ulcer's playing up, I don't feel well.'

'What! Oh, this is the final bloody straw. You're going to let the town down?'

'You've already said my job's as good as gone, why should *I* give a bugger? Let a relief man come in. Let's see how he copes with your "Mrs Calvary, Dog Rock".'

'I thought you had more in you than this, D'Arce.'

'*Noblesse oblige?* I expect I have, for despite your false and vicious accusations, I'll report for duty next Sunday night. Good evening, Miss Pruvagol, sleep well. I'll be round for some Tagamet later.'

'Good night, D'Arce. No hard feelings?'

'By the way, D'Arcy, your vehicle's blowing smoke. You'd better have it seen to.'

I think I did the right thing getting out of town for a few days. Every time I arrive home lately, Rochesters' lights go out and the curtains open. Now, let's have a look at this map, and keep your eyes peeled for wheat. That's right, wheat! As eaten by parrots. If you see a little trail of wheat, of the kind Hansel and Gretel could have made, let me know.

We'll take the swamp by the Hell Hole first. God only

knows what's in this park, the ranger never goes off the track. I think at this stage it's important we have a word with Terry Derry. I've made a few inquiries about him and I didn't learn much, except that he was a very good hockey player, who went off to war at eighteen. He served in New Guinea, but what became of him there, no one seems to know. He stopped writing home for a time, but then his mother received an unsigned, typewritten letter from him, or supposedly from him, postmarked Rabaul, in which he said he would be coming back, but he wouldn't want to see her. The feeling is, he was badly disfigured, he was very vain about his good looks. Anyway, he left notes for his mother, typewritten, in the stall, from time to time. For my part, I wish more people in this town would learn to use a typewriter: it would make my job easier. Our news-agent is the worst culprit: I defy any man on earth to read his postcodes. Anything from him goes straight in my re-sort bundle. Derry must know this park like the back of his hand. You don't get any yellow box till fifty miles from here, and the spotted gum is down on the coast, so Derry works the non-commercial species like river peppermint and rough-barked apple most bee men don't bother with.

Hey, that was a bee! Did you see it go by? It was heading over that hill, give us the map.

Well, the swamp's the other way, but we best follow the bee.

I have the feeling Derry may be a prickly sort of cove. Beekeeping does that to some people, it's like karate. The local yobbos who learn karate – there's a class twice a week in the hall, conducted by a man with such big arms he can't reach his cheeks to shave them – become real gentlemen, but there's always that one or two who go the other way entirely. They're the ones you see in action outside the bottom pub sportsman's bar, Friday night. Most beekeepers I have known were Church of England ministers, but I'm thinking if you don't mix with old women, if you lived out here in the scrub on your own, nursing grievances against mankind with only bees for company: I might point out that

Munich in the early part of this century was the world centre for honeybee research. Yes, they can be vicious. Yes, they will happily rob other hives and fight to the death to protect their own. An individual life means nothing to them, and I could go on, but I won't, except to say they'd have very little time for the bee equivalents of bludgers and poofters.

Something else about them, too: they always kill a maimed or injured queen, to be on the safe side.

Now he must have a local contact, and since his mother died, he has no family here. I expect we'll find a pile of whisky bottles like the one outside the Inna-mincka pub, but he needs wire and he needs foundation comb, unless he's got his bees in hollow logs. Someone has to buy him his tins, and I've checked out all the apiary suppliers, and they know nothing of him. The only Dog Rock addresses they have on their books are Ursula Topwaite's and my own, and they don't recall a disfigured man, or one who wore a veil into the shop. It could be Hiram, it could be a Balthazar, it could be any-one from the ashram. We'll ask. And while we're in his camp, keep your eyes peeled for the typewriter, and any old pile of magazines.

Well, the bees are getting thicker. Ti-tree's early this year. They're working the ti-tree on the other side of that swamp, which is a good mile from here. Burning fuel to do it too, it makes me wonder what Derry's on about. There's an apiary up ahead, all right: too many bees for the odd wild hive.

He'd have to move them about, surely.

It's getting dark. I wonder if we shouldn't camp here for the night and press on in the morning. Seems funny to be camping where you can still hear the trains on the Main Western Line, but he's not the sort of man I feel I'd want to disturb on a dark night. Just joking, he's bound to have a portable tele: he'd heard of Xavier Morgan.

Let's get the Paddy Pallin Tassie tent up then.

Well, there they are. And just as we expected, not a trace of Derry. Keep away from those hives: they're a vicious stock, you'll recall. That'd be the hive that went up to the stables; the little one, over there. You could carry that, with a bit of effort. You wouldn't carry one of those three-deckers. It's backbreaking work, is bee-keeping. I knew a man had to load and unload 190 of those, three times in less than a mile one dark night, when his truck got bogged in wet sandhills. And they don't like being banged about, either.

This is where Derry must have dossed, in this little beehive hut. There's his typewriter, and there's his television. Good God, he's got a video recorder. Will you look at the size of that ghetto blaster? And aren't those bloodstains on the typewriter? We'd better go back and get the Sergeant.

'Now as you can see, Sergeant, his hives are still gummed up from winter. The honey that's being sold at the stall, the bloodstains on the typewriter; it looks like murder to me.'

'*Murder* you reckon? But what's the motive and where's the corpse?'

'Notice anything about the hives, Sergeant?'

'Apart from being stolen, they've been painted brown and green.'

'Look at those six four-deckers over there, sitting all on their own. How far apart would you say they were?'

'Oh, not more than three or four feet.'

'And the ground around them has been disturbed. No bee man puts a permanent apiary as close together as that. The workers would drift, and a young queen returning from her mating flight could well enter the wrong hive and be killed. Someone, not a bee man, has put those hives there, from which it follows, as surely as meringues follow a hollandaise sauce on the menu at the Bonny Tops RSL dining room, there's something buried under them.'

'One way to find out. Shift'em and take a look! Got your veil handy, D'Arce?'

'Do you think you could get a vehicle in here?'

'No way.'

'There's 300 pounds in a four-decker hive. I can't see you and me lumping six of them a mile to the nearest track. God knows how Derry managed.'

'What do you mean? Stick them over there with the others would do quite nicely, you can drag them, can't you?'

'Sergeant: the worker bee locates her hive by position. If we were to shift those bees less than three miles, the foragers would keep returning.'

'They'll have to be killed. They've no business being in this park in the first place. Besides which, they're all stolen. Stolen over a period of years. I checked the brands with the Ag Dept.'

'They've *every* business being here. They've been on this continent since 1822, which is a long time by Australian standards. And as to being stolen, have a heart! All bees are inveterate thieves. I'm sure Derry only stole hives when his bees were robbing one another. There is another way: if the hives are moved daily, less than one foot at a time . . .'

'Right, that's settled. Give me a shout when they're all moved. In the meantime, I'll get going. The mail should be sorted by now.'

Between you and me, I'll bet a quid these bees saw Derry being murdered. It's not a sight they'd have enjoyed either. I'm starting to think Derry knew more about bees than the minister at Moreton-in-the-Marsh. There's no sign at all of a smoker or veil, as though he didn't need them, never used them.

'Sergeant! You'll have to get a helicopter to spray that apiary. I've never been stung so hard in my entire life. Those are one-man bees. Besides, it'll take me a fortnight to shift the hives a foot a day, and I'm taking my annual leave from October the first.'

'Okay, D'Arcy, I'll see what we can do. Start a little fire, might be the shot. You want to read the Ripper's confession while you're here?'

'No I certainly don't. The Ripper must have heard of that first murder and thought to himself, I'll continue with this. The first murder occurred on a Tuesday night, a Tuesday night! Now what does *that* suggest? Never mind, I put it to you the first had nothing in common with the rest.'

'Ah, but I have in front of me . . .'

'A confession that's not worth a meadow argus to a butterfly collector, beg pardon. The false confession of a desperately confused, guilt-ridden, psychopathic killer. Believe me when I say the pattern is wrong.'

'And why should I believe you? And when are you going back on the run?'

'Fair go, I can't do my work and your work and Derry's work as well! If things were as they should be, I shouldn't have to work at *all!*'

'You'll find that sort of attitude cuts no ice out here.'

'Why were all the murders committed when I was on days? And why did the shutter fall and how? And who put the bees in Hathaway's stables? And who murdered Terry Derry, assuming Terry Derry *was* murdered? And who moved the hives? Who poisoned the horses and doped the dog? Who hired Hamburger's truck? Now that's something you *could* find out! And who hid the wombat in the long grass? And who mailed the implement to me, or tried to make it look as though it had been? Have you the answer to *any* of these questions?'

'So it *was* mailed to you? And I suppose you removed the address.'

'I expect it was addressed to me, because that way I'd have had to explain why it was in my possession. I have the very strong feeling I'd handled that parcel before. By the way, what's the time?'

'Five past four. Why?'

'I have an appointment with Dr Opfinger and I want to speak to the travel agent.'

I was *so* looking forward to the Cotswold Way, and now I doubt I'll even see it. All those months of preparation gone in vain. All those deposits forfeited. I can see no way out of a twelve-day Best of Britain Trafalgar Tour, and a seven-day Best of Scotland Trafalgar Tour, and a seventeen-day Traditional Europe Trafalgar Tour, and God help the poor buggers sitting next to me. Even as I speak, someone is dreaming of a beautiful holiday I am bound to ruin.

━━━━

7 Miss Kareer will see us shortly.

I suppose we drove through some of the most fertile grazing land in the state, on our way here, and what's on it, horses apart, but a handful of mangy Hereford cows and a dozen billy goats. It's gone out of production and the real farmers have moved to less productive land. Did you see all the Land for Sale signs? I don't think there's a self-respecting dairyman hereabouts who hasn't parcelled up and sold off, at ten times its value, every block his ancestors sweated to clear that fronts a bitumen road. One time I could put a face to every private boxholder. Now, I wouldn't know one from another and there's two more a month. We're running out of private boxes. Three hundred and fifty hobby farms within five miles of the PO! The Dalgleish Pastoral Company; that's a five-acre block that happened to inherit a cowcrush, and so on.

If I may generalize, these pioneers – the ones that lie down on the rusty barbed-wire fences for the next wave to trample over – are desperate and sensitive urban people, unable to cope with city neighbours. They drive up to Hrubucek's estate on the weekend, and the family admire the view, something old Calvary, who worked that land till he couldn't walk, never did once in his entire life – he was always staring at the feed, scrutinizing the sub-clover – and they think to themselves, 'This is for us.' You see them later in the Zinnia, scoffing gem scones and wearing that queer, bedazzled expression city folk assume when they're being harangued by some boring yokel, and before you can say 'Think twice', he's bought a home computer and she's reading books on how to grow herbs and they've sold their house and made the plunge.

I give them ten years. They have no skills, no family support system, precious little capital, no clan. They'll learn the hard way that beautiful surroundings do nothing to change the nature of man: one of the meanest men I ever met was a Nepalese Ghurkha from under Annapurna. They see their herb farm failing through no fault of their own, and their son turning into a rustic lout whose chief entertainment is chasing his mates up and down the platform at the railway station with a bumper hanging from the corner of his mouth, but, in the nature of things, others will buy what they can't make work, and their life had meaning for a time, and no one can say they didn't try, as though trying counted for anything.

Rural communities are formed by blood ties over many generations. What we have here is not the birth of something, but the death of something else entirely. I speak as one who's seen it before. This is the metastasis of a cancer, spreading from the arse and the wide-open mouth and hunting out the liver. This is the way civilizations die, read your Gibbons on the Fall of Rome. As the rector says, we don't know whether we're up, down, strange, charming or beauty-flavoured, and the last thing I feel like looking at is the future, in the form of tourist Europe. But I've no doubt we'll find there the key to the mystery, or at least, I hope we do.

'Mr D'Oliveres! You're not here to tell me you want to change the date on your ticket again?'

'No, Miss Kareer, it's nothing serious. Old Bert Arblaster's been singing the praises of Trafalgar Tours to me, and I wonder if it's still possible to book myself in for a tour or two.'

'I think you're being very wise. It *is* a lot cheaper and a lot less trouble than doing things on your own. Now is it the Money Stretcher or Cost Saver you think might interest you?'

'Which one did Bert take?'

'Nothing but the best for Mr Arblaster! He and his wife did the Top Tours.'

'And is there much difference in price?'

'Well, naturally. The Top Tours give you private facilities in mainly first-class hotels, but all tours provide the services of a professional tour manager, and your TT travel bag, containing your map and travel booklets, will be supplied.'

'I suppose I'll do what Bert did. I'm still in time I hope?'

'Let's take a look. Do you want to do Britain, Scotland or Europe?'

'How about the Isle of Man? A TT tour of the Isle of Man: can that be organized?'

'October *is* the end of the season. And don't forget Mr and Mrs Arblaster made two separate trips. On their first trip, from memory, they did the Best of Britain and Traditional Europe, and on their second the Best of Scotland only. Trafalgar Tours don't do Northern Ireland or the Isle of Man.'

'Put me down for the Best of Britain. Is there a tour leaving on the second of October?'

'Let me check. From memory, the Best of Britain coaches leave London on Sundays, Tuesdays and Fridays . . . oh, but look: in October, they only leave on Sundays. That gives you a week in London.'

'What a pest. Can't I do Traditional Europe in that time?'

'Goodness me no! You can't do Traditional Europe in a week, it takes a full seventeen days.'

'Then what about the Best of Scotland? That wouldn't take long, surely?'

'Those tours leave on a Sunday too. No, I'm afraid you'll just have to put up with a week in London to begin with. Would you like to stay at a Trafalgar hotel?'

'I think I'd best. Do any of these Trafalgar Tours call at Cape Trafalgar?'

'Do please be sensible, Mr D'Oliveres. The cheapest Trafalgar hotel in London is the Tara Hotel, in Kensington.'

'I guess Bert stayed at the most expensive.'

'No, actually he *did* stay at the Tara, I couldn't get them into the Cumberland. I'll be able to get you into the

Tara in October, and here's an idea: why not take the Trafalgar Tours Seven Nights in London package? The price includes seven nights' accommodation with continental breakfast, a London theatre ticket . . .'

'I don't want to see *The Mousetrap*. Mrs Arblaster tells me Bert complained all the way through it.'

'. . . a sightseeing tour of London . . .'

'I want to see the house where David Bowie was born.'

'. . . *and* your choice of an evening with the stars at the London Room, or an unforgettable five-course medieval banquet at the Beefeater, or a sparkling Scottish cabaret at the Caledonian, including, if you're game to wear one, a free kilt and sporran.'

'If I'm game to wear one! Have you seen me in my masonic regalia? Thank you, but even if it does cost more, I'll book into the hotel in the normal way. I'm prepared to pay an extra ten quid to miss out on a Caledonian cabaret.'

'Mr and Mrs Arblaster went to the medieval feast.'

'My dear Miss Kareer: I *do* have a mind of my own, and could you give me Bert's itinerary? That would make things easier.'

I'm going back to work for the rest of the week. Cadwalloper went ahead and burned those hives, with the ranger's acquiescence, and I'm that upset, I'm frightened I could speak out of turn were my hands not fully occupied. There's not much you can give a bee in return for honey, outside of a home, and burning those hives . . . well, I'd just as soon not think about it. I do hope none of the queens survived.

The remains of Derry's dismembered body, or parts of it, were found under the hives, if it *was* Derry's body: the head, the torso, an arm and two legs, and under one hive, his smoker and hive tool. They'd only been there a couple of months – still had flesh attached – and they're treating it as murder, well, they would do. I dare say they'll try to pin it on me, but maybe there's no need for that now.

I read somewhere the autopsy has declined in medical popularity. Diagnosis of death proves faulty in 40 per cent of cases. I have reasons for thinking Derry wasn't murdered, but I'll keep them to myself, for the time being.

If Derry was murdered, I'll be murdered too.

Speaking of pathology and medical malpractice, we'll visit Isbester this weekend. He's an oncologist as well as a Brahmin breeder, so when he's not producing beef for our tables, he's working on cures for our cancers of the colon. I want to check with Cassandra, his wife, on how the rice-growing is going along. I'm very interested to learn who gave her the idea of growing rice in the first place. If it's all right with you then, we'll meet in my kitchen first thing Saturday morning.

Well, I'd expected it and hoped for it, but when it came I was unprepared. Things happen so quickly when you come off that bike, you don't have time to consider.

There are only three sections on the beat where I get the throttle open: when I'm returning from Cow Flat Road, when I'm closing in on Ghostloaf Grange and when I'm climbing the hill from Arblasters. I'd always thought if someone wanted to run me off the road, they'd do it there. It's only a 110 cc bike, but I've had it sitting on 80 kph, and when you wrap yourself round a tree at 80 kph, you usually feel, phew, that was close, but in the ambulance you go into shock and you're dead on arrival at the hospital (DOA). Ruptured aorta: that's the way bikies die that wrap themselves round trees.

Imagine then my great surprise, as I was rounding the right-hand corner onto the overhead bridge by the fire station, to feel the bike dig in and prop, at the same time flinging me upwards and off. I must have been doing 40 kph and I hit the ground on my bad knee and rolled. I'll pull my kneeguard off; you can see the gravel rash for yourself. This is the knee I hurt as a lad, fell-running in the Dales. I was always last to the top of the peaks, but first across the line. No one could catch me running down the hills. Just as well I wasn't banking on the Cotswold Way, I can barely walk now.

But that's not all of it: I hit the ground on my bad knee and rolled. Took all the skin off my hands, I can't lift the blessed kettle to make a cup of tea, would you mind? I must have rolled at least twice before I hit the fence post, and the fence post was so rotten it snapped off at the base, and my whole body went through the fence sideways, with the exception of my head, which, because of my helmet, got jammed under the lowest strand of wire. I was left dangling over the down line, being slowly asphyxiated. I had the first bundle for Loftus Street in my left hand, as far as Calvary's *Australian Stock Horse*, and I remember dropping it, as a train went by beneath me. It landed in the back of an empty S-truck, so it shouldn't be too hard to track down. It says volumes for this town's compassion, their chief concern is that bundle of missing mail. According to some, it contained an important letter and cheque for Mrs Livermore. Now anyone with a franking machine will claim the letter's in the mail: frankly, I don't remember seeing it. I couldn't climb back up with the bundle, and anyway, they'll issue another cheque I'm sure. If you want your letter to be treated as though it were posted in Japan, take my advice, and send it registered mail or priority paid.

The bike hit the brick pylon on the bridge: I did the front forks in completely. If we can't get another bike, Fargo will have to deliver the mail next week from his Hudson, unless he's prepared to take the pushbike out, and I haven't seen the handlebars since last year's school frolic, when little Aggie Hardacre borrowed them as part of an headdress for an Indian chief.

It was as I was rolling I heard the car, and I vaguely recall a glimpse of some hubs, but beyond that, my mind's a blank. I know now how Fargo must have felt, when he hit that wombat. By the time I climbed back up to the road, I was shaking like a boy caught in a orchard. Even if I'd had the presence of mind to inspect the bike, a crowd of pensioners were gathered round it, and any one of them could have interfered with it.

Wouldn't you think they'd have looked for me? I'd like to think they assumed I'd been found, but the Sergeant last year pulled a man from a crashed car, who'd been sitting there a night and a day in full view of every person travelling to and from the limestone works.

I was sent to hospital for observation, but they let me out after three hours. Only one thing could have caused the accident: the right-hand sidestand must have been down.

Now I never use a right-hand sidestand: being British, I lean a bike to the left and I can't adapt to innovation. This is the first bike we've had at the PO even had two sidestands. I found the chunk out of the tarmac where the stand dug in as I was cornering. I cut the corner a bit. You know what the Sergeant said? He intends to book me on two counts: one, crossing double yellow lines, and two, reckless riding.

Well, that's it for me, then: I'll lose my licence, and there's my job gone. It's the policy, in these days of unemployment, a postie must have a clean bike licence. Every bike rider in the place cuts that corner, but it's me cops the bluey. I don't think they're trying to lose me my job, though, so much as kill me, at this stage.

The car that almost crushed me was American, accelerating as it hit the bridge. I'd say it had been lurking round the corner, waiting for the sound of my approach. It missed me by no more than inches: thirty seconds earlier, and I'd have gone under. I dare say they didn't think an old chap like me would hit that corner so hard, but I wanted to watch the *Mike Walsh Show*, as he was supposed to be interviewing Lord Lew Grade, with whom I've had a few exchanges. When you come off a bike on a corner, your fate is in the lap of the gods: if you've room to slide, you may get out of it, as I did, with a few abrasions or a fracture: if a car's coming and you hit it head on, you're dead, or better off dead.

By George, it happens quickly. If I could have noted the rego on that car, when it was passing my ear as I was rolling . . . oh well, it's easy to think of what you should have done after the event. The District Postal Superintendent wants an explanation as to why I was clutching mail. I've half a mind to take the last week off, but my budget's tight, because of those Tours. Miss Kareer rang this morning, she's squeezed me in on all three. I can't walk anyway.

The worst of it is, that's the first solid right-hand corner I hit at any speed on the run. My right-hand sidestand could have been lowered for me at any of 147 drops.

They're saying I'm just a careless oaf. Only one person believes me. Wayne Mercaptan! He rang last night from the Plymouth signal box, God how word spreads.

'I knew,' he said, 'as soon as I heard, who must have been driving that car'; and he went on to discuss the run-ins he's had with the man in the black Chevy Corvette. He could have something: I've been wondering why I can't think of the colour of that car to save my job. If it were black, that could account for it. I checked it out with the sergeant, and he confirmed what I've often suspected: there's not a black car in this town or for miles around, except for my Jowett Javelin.

Right, let's get to the Masterpiece. I hope you'll excuse the state of my kitchen. I intend to give it a proper spring cleaning when I return from Hong Kong. I'll change the fat in the baking pan then, and scrub out the whole stove.

I want to call by at Arblaster's, she wants to make marmalade from my oranges. I think old Bert does care for her, despite what everyone says. He went home the other day with half a dozen odd saucers he'd found at the fete – 'Thought you might be able to use these,' he says, throwing them on the table – it's his offhanded manner misleads people. It's true, though, something's not right in the marriage and it shows in the attitude of the children. You never see them, for one thing. They got away from Labour-in-Vain as quick as ever they could. Ross, he's the eldest, he's always talking about what he'd do if his wife and kids were killed in an accident. Bonny's as mean as her old man: I can remember Bert in the PO once, trying to tear a piece off an oversize postcard. 'Damn,' he says, 'I think Mum's written on the back.' The counter must be jumping up there, with no one knowing who's on the run, but it's worse when the PM takes a day off: everyone wants to know where he is, and if he's ill, what's wrong with him. 'Ron ill?' 'No, his father died.' How would you like to relieve a PM and have to say that a hundred times a day? I said to the last bloke, I said, you ought to write it down on a bloody blackboard. And when he's ill, they want to know his blood pressure: I generally ring the hospital after I read the rain gauge.

I feed my oranges on sulphate of ammonia and cull the dead wood religiously, or should I say, irreligiously. The navel comes in first, then the Valencias. Five good months I get. All that nut grass I dug up to plant them, I broke it by hand to a depth of three feet. Having rid myself of it, I had an inspiration: why not go the whole hog and plant a lawn? So I borrowed the heavy roller from the club. I remember the night I came home from a meeting early, as I'd seen the downpour coming – the topsoil and all the seed met me at the front gate. I got the shovel and the wheelbarrow and shovelled it all back in and spread it, till dawn was breaking. Two weeks later, up it came, and nutgrass! Nary a one.

What do you like by way of photos? Cakes and caravans are my favourites, but nowdays, with everyone travelling the globe, I'm hardly game to ask to see any. Bert's one of these people who doesn't own a camera, so he buys books of postcards wherever he goes, and cuts them out and mounts them in albums. He showed me a photo of the Trooping of the Colour and told me it was Bastille Day in Copenhagen. He'd cut the label off, to make it look as though he'd taken the photo himself.

I'm honorary colonel of the Old Two-Tone Blues, I'll bet you'd never have guessed.

'Shocking thing about Derry, D'Arcy.'

'Shocking thing, Bert. Here's the oranges for the missus. How's it going on the farm?'

'They're here this weekend, the cheesecloth's flying. We've been drafting cattle all morning. Now I maintain a man shouldn't have to be told you don't draft cattle down a hill, and he still has to look between their legs to see if they're cows or bulls. All he's learned is the names of the grasses: they must know the names of those grasses.'

'It would be instructive to hear the conversation at a tea room in a hospital, Bert.'

'He wanted me to give his registrars a talk on cattle, but when you get old you get cunning. They couldn't meet my fee. I charge like a wounded buffalo now.'

'I'm on my way over to see them.'

'Why would you want to see them?'

'If you look at the map, their bottom paddock is the closest to where Derry's body was found. Someone had to be supplying Derry.'

'Now you listen to me, D'Arcy: I don't know why you feel you have to buy maps and involve yourself in everything that goes on around here, but take my advice and keep your nose clean. Stop trying to do the copper's job. Beulah Livermore is most upset about losing her cheque; she had an oil payment due.'

'You don't understand, Bert.'

'I understand all too well your mind's not on your job. I heard you doped Fargo's dog. I heard you poisoned Miss Hathaway's horses, just because her shutter kept falling. Now I can pick malicious rumours, but plenty can't, and I have to warn you a campaign is being mounted to have you transferred when the old exchange closes.'

'I can't compete with a man born and bred in Dog Rock, Bert; I understand that.'

'You're a far more conscientious postman than Fargo, but you're losing your advantage. Every time you stick your big bib in where it's not required, you lose another vote. Take the advice of an older man, son: rest up, enjoy your holiday, and come back here with a change of attitude. Have you been watching the weather over there?'

'Why would I? There's nothing I can do about it.'

'And don't go poking about this place.'

'Are you threatening me, Bert?'

'See what I mean? Can't be spoken to! Won't listen to reason.'

I've a fair idea why he doesn't want us poking about Idle-a-While. Some of the works he's countenanced here are an absolute disgrace. Who ever heard of building bullpens with timber dressed all round? And that big silo, ready for the rice crop: that must have cost a pretty penny.

'Cassandra Isbester?'

'That's right. Who are you?'

'An admirer of your appearance and initiative. I won't keep you, just wanted to ask who put you onto growing rice. I've been telling the locals here for years . . .'

'Who is it, bub?'

'I didn't catch the name.'

'Just the local postman.'

'He's not local! I looked up his surname in the phone-book and it's the only one. Come on in, D'Arce! I'm Mal; it is D'Arce, isn't it? Whisky, D'Arce? Know of any jobs going? I'm lookin' for something a bit more handy.'

'But surely, a good oncologist . . .'

'No more medicine for me, cob; I'm gettin' *out* o' that rat race! I quite like breedin' Brahmins, got a natural flair. Must have, eh? Been asked to judge'm at next year's Royal, 'smatterof fact. But I don't want to get too big, you know? Just want a piece of what *you've* got, D'Arcy: a life of meaning and contentment! There's a few workin' years in me yet, mate. I own this place now, did you know?'

'Bert told me.'

'I had nothin' to start with, D'Arce, come up the hard way, wrong side of the Spit Bridge. Done all right though, made a quid. 'Nother whisky?'

'Thank you. House of Lords, I see.'

'Just meself and the missus here and the lad and young Balthazar – hey, look at him, D'Arce, he's *craw-lin'*! This place'll be his one day. Give us a break, Mal, he's saying. Look at his toothy big grin, eh D'Arce? Got any nippers yourself, mate? He's actually my great-grandson. Always been a terror for the birds.'

'No, Mal, I was never married.'

'Good for you. I been married five, six times is it, Cass? Why I got bugger-all. What do you think of me latest and best though, D'Arce? Nice norks, eh? Too good for me. They say there's no fool like an old fool, D'Arcy, by crikey, I think they're right. But I don't want to sit round

138

here all day guarding her. I want to get out and *work*. I want to get out and find the job I was meant for, while there's still time.'

'You'll find there's work around a farm.'

'I pay Bert to do that.'

'Do you *have* to work, Mal?'

'I was never meant to be a quack, I'm a *worker* mate, look at these hands! Amongst the fencepost you and I, I've only five years to find my true vocation.'

'And what do you think of all this, Cassandra? Are *you* in favour of Mal's working?'

'Why shouldn't Mal find happiness, D'Arcy? If he wants to work on the railways . . .'

'He's not going to work on the *railways?*'

'I'm not proud, D'Arce. Going for me interview next week. Track maintenance gang.'

'But this is preposterous! What about the unemployed?'

'They won't work on the maintenance gang. Wouldn't work in an iron lung, most of 'em. You ask the ganger, what's his name? Had the vacancy in at the CES over three months. They come out, work a day, that's it. Never sees 'em again.'

'Who put you onto growing rice, Cassandra? I know you haven't actually started yet.'

'I think it was Mal's idea, wasn't it, Mal?'

'Who says you can't grow rice here, D'Arcy? Has anyone given it a go? We Aussies gotta make every post a *winning* post. Gotta put these swamps to work. I made an offer years back for this place. Knew he'd come round eventually.'

I intend to speak to the ganger and tell him who Isbester is. Bert must have seen him coming. *I* would have seen him coming. I'd hate to tell you what he paid for 200 acres of paperbark swamp, but I find it interesting the offer was made long before Bert took it up.

You know why they come to the country? It's the one place modern marriage can survive. If you're lucky enough to have a wife, that is; the worst of my job is, I don't get the chance to meet unmarried women under sixty.

139

That last observation came to me as a flash of blinding insight. Blame it on the House of Lords Scotch whisky, which is now steering me towards the manager's cottage and the Balthazars' residence. No!

Keep it quiet, will you? We'll check the greenhouse, something funny going on there. Anyone home? Can't see a light. What's tonight? Saturday night. Bush band should be playing, by rights. Could be Malbane's home though: not a real good night on the cabs, wages are all gone. Thursday night and Friday night are the big nights in Bonny Tops.

Door to the hothouse locked? No. Moon's coming out, you beauty. What can we see? Blessed tomato plants everywhere, but look! A sawhorse. A router, some netting. There's a pile of little boxes on the floor. Lift one up, so I can look at it.

I'll be blessed, who'd have guessed it? A tiny, collapsible *bird*cage! Wait a minute: there's no door and one side has no netting. I always knew this pair were into something dishonest, but I thought it was pirate cassettes. Ask yourself this: the hand-eye coordination developed in pinball parlours, what use to a grown man? Malbane is the number one customer for the small, padded postal bookbag.

Oh.

'Grab him, Dodger! Got him? Hey, wait a minute, it's a cop!'

'No, it's not, he's wearing shorts. It's that nosy postman.'

'Oh yeah, I recognize him now. Into the house, you! What are you after? We could have you done for breaking and entering.'

'Call the police then.'

'We don't need the police. We'll take care of this ourselves. We ought to give you a damn good hiding. What were you looking for out there?'

'Lost my way. Visiting Isbesters. Too drunk to drive home.'

'Yeah? A likely story. You've had your eyes on that greenhouse.'

140

'Ask your cobber to unhand me. My arms are very sore.'

'I tell you mate, you'll have more than sore arms if you go round wearing a blue uniform.'

'I haven't had time to change!'

'That only makes matters worse, from a distance. Now we want no trouble. You saw nothing and you know nothing, got that?'

'I saw what I saw and I know what I know. All right, I'll take you into my confidence. Whose idea was it, your building those small collapsible birdcages, which is what they would be, with another piece of netting attached and a door?'

'Smell his breath, Dodger.'

'I'm talking about the little cages on the hothouse floor in there.'

'He means the *tree* guards. All right, if it's any business of yours, we're devising a system to protect fruit trees from birds, without the use of harmful chemicals. Those are just mock-ups.'

'That's what *you* think! In point of fact, they are the object of the exercise. I'll tell you why, if you'll unhand me. Thank you: now I'll start with a question: what do we have within five miles of this lovely village of ours, which is one of the most rare, valuable, priceless and costly things in the whole world?'

'Peace and quiet. Fresh air.'

'I'm speaking of something money can *buy*. Here's a clue: it flies on green wings in the dead of night.'

'He's off the air, Malbane.'

'Shut up! What are you talking about postie? Stop speaking in riddles.'

'The swamp parrot. It's an extremely rare parrot, one of three ground-living parrots in the world. It flies by night. It lives in the park here. I have heard it, "Tee tee stit, tee tee stit, tee tee tee stit". Buttongrass seed eater. Looks just like a night parrot. Ever heard of the night parrot?'

'Should never drink when you're concussed.'

'Shut up, he's making good sense. Night parrot, how much worth dollars?'

141

'Name your price, to certain unscrupulous continental students of ornithology. Only one known specimen
has ever been taken, in 1868, from the arid Gawler
Ranges. It was sent, for some reason, to Melbourne and
the German botanist Baron von Mueller, who figured on
the 1951 twopenny-halfpenny postage stamp. He sent it
to the London Zoo.'

'Oh no!'

'I'm afraid so. It lived there a full four months, before
dying of pneumonia in January.'

'It's not enough they lock us up and send us over
here!'

'Not one single specimen has been sighted since
1883. It is believed extinct. Its closest living relative is
this local swamp parrot, now almost equally rare. Yet I
have heard it. Both birds are dumpy, nocturnal ground
dwellers, green with yellow and black streaks. Their
chief distinction is their choice of habitat; it occurs to me
this would be irrelevant in a cage. An unscrupulous
dealer could well pass one off as the other.'

'And what would a night parrot be worth?'

'Name your price, to certain unscrupulous continental sufferers from insomnia. Collecting birds would
seem to be one of man's most powerful instincts. I judge
it to be innate. Take the boy who keeps a budgie in a
cage – the best known Aussie of them all, the budgie –
intensify and heighten the instinct through generations
of chook fancying and gamecock breeding; educate; add
a doctorate, a pince-nez, a warped sense of honour and
generations of ill-gotten gains . . . suffice it to say there
are men who would part with a million dollars for less.'

'A million dollars!'

'For a single specimen: a breeding pair would no
doubt fetch more. Are you aware what the common
galah will fetch on the streets of Amsterdam?'

'It sounds as though *you* are: I don't like this,
Malbane. He's supposed to be a duke.'

'What nonsense. Only a baron, the lowest rank of the
peerage, and a penniless one at that. But if I were plan-
ning an international parrot smuggling ring, boys, I'd

142

work the racket from here. Come on lads, who put you up to it? Don't think I don't know it was *her!*'

'Tell him nothing, he sounds like a crook. That postal uniform is a front.'

'Was it her put you up to it?'

'Oh no: someone else is at the door now!'

'Could be Silas and Bronwyn.'

'I'm leaving.'

'You stay where you are! Dodger, open the door please.'

Well well well, if it's not my lead and number three from the number three Pennants.

Fancy Bert trying to have me booked for trespass: I can't see us playing in the State Pairs now. I had a lawful reason for being on Idle-a-While, and when I was asked to leave, I went. The lads, to their credit, said they'd asked me in for a cup of tea and an Iced Vovo.

He doesn't even own it anyway: it belongs to Mal Isbester now.

Of course I know it's not *her*, I just can't have anyone thinking I know what I'm doing at this late stage. I know you promised you'd keep it to yourself, but I can't take the risk. I can't have Renee, Carmel & Co spreading it round town, it's too dangerous.

He couldn't have rung the Sergeant, he hasn't got the phone on. So he walked up, through Hathaways. I wonder did he overhear us talking together in the paddock. He must have followed us to Isbester's place, and waited outside till we left.

It was quite an honour for him to be asked to play in the State Pairs with me: he was proud as Punch initially. And yet he's prepared to cruel an opportunity I'll see doesn't come his way again. And Cadwalloper must have known he couldn't book me – unless Bert overheard what went on, when we got sprung in the hothouse by those boys.

The old bugger: so he must have been following us all round that paddock. But he made a mistake in thinking Mal's tenants would work in with the law: they're true blue, if not two-tone.

What's today? Sunday. I wish I got to London on Sunday. Early Sunday morning I could take the double-decker bus, there'd be no one on it but me: I'm always first through customs. The oaks and elms would restore my equanimity. The city would be so quiet. I'd pass by the Thames, and see young middle-class women walking Great Dane dogs over freshly painted bridges. In a way, I'm glad you won't be coming. I need some time to myself.

I know the sense of relief I'll feel, even on a Tuesday. It's a shameful feeling, but I know I'll feel it. Even Bert said *he* felt it, and he's a fifth-generation Australian. You feel like someone who's been under stress they haven't been able to show; a woman, nursing a fractious invalid; a farmer, struggling through seven years of drought; a young mum, saddled with boisterous brats, whose grandparents won't lift a finger to help. But at last, the old bugger's passed away, or rain's falling, the kids are off to school, and you find yourself sitting at the kitchen table, bawling your bloody eyes out. It's never quite as bad for me, as I have the run of two hemispheres. My main concern at this stage is losing my precious passport. You see the way they're trying to nail me? Trespass, reckless riding; that's why I wouldn't drive the car home last night. Booked for drunken driving, I'd be gone. Thank God I survived a week on the run! I can walk to the exchange, and I'm staying in this kitchen at other times, with the door locked. I won't answer the phone. I'll tell Fargo to hold my mail. If I had any money I'd book myself in at the Airport Hilton and stay there the week.

I received a letter from the warden at the hostel at Stow-on-the-Wold, Friday. He confirmed my booking, but I shan't be seeing Stow this trip. Day One we head for Plymouth, where Francis Drake played a famous game of bowls, via Stonehenge (tales of druids and sun worship), Hardy's Dorset and Exeter Cathedral. Day Twelve, our last day, we inspect Wroxton, before visiting Blenheim; that's as close as I'll get to my ancestral home.

144

I recall clearly the last time I walked the Cotswold Way, it was very wet. The sky was black; great dark clouds were rolling over, it was colder than spring here. I walked myself beyond endurance; that's the purpose of long-distance walking. I came out the other side of exhaustion between Scottsquar Hill and Standish Wood. I remember the moment precisely. I'd managed to get myself lost earlier – a farmer had planted wheat on the track – and my soaking wet pack was weighing me down, and I'd bruised my foot the night before, sweeping the stairs at Duntisbourne Abbotts, but I kept wading on through the mud and the frequent torrential downpours of rain, as though I had an important dispatch for my Queen, and suddenly the clouds rolled back, and the sun shone through, and I knew at once why I was there, and that this whole life of mine is just a bad dream. I can't seem to do that here, I've tried, but it doesn't work. I don't feel I've any great stake in the place. It doesn't seem to matter if I stop walking, or walk on. An endurance walker needs to carry a powerful image in his mind; it's a form of meditation, really. In my case, I think of my ancestors.

Balthazar Whitefriar wrote a poem once, on the back of a kangaroo postcard, in which he complained that jet travel and foreign television programmes conspire to give him the feeling, wherever he goes, of an unseen companion, just out of sight. He said he never feels alone, even in the Simpson Desert. He always has the feeling a David Attenborough camera crew will appear at any moment, from behind the nearest sandhill.

Have you seen the face on the likes of Bert walking down the Strand? It's the face of a young Balthazar in the Court of the Crimson King. 'Invisibles' – the chains they can't see – are what keep us Brits in the black.

Do you know why I'm doing this thing I'm doing? I've given out as much as I dare. It all began when I bought this house, the perfect house for a parrot smuggler. Over the gully from a man with a million chooks, surrounded by high Mexican pines. All I wanted was privacy, and the consolations of a quiet life. I took what I thought to be an honest job, but couldn't quite settle in, couldn't quite knuckle down. No, I had to go back to Britain every blessed year, and through that weakness, I've set myself up, and fully deserve what I'm getting.

À outrance! To the Bitter End! That's my family motto, and I'm the last of the male line. I could have married, if I'd wanted.

And why else would I go back to Britain every year, but to smuggle out parrots? I'm always walking in the park, aren't I, with a pair of bird-watching binoculars?

Did you hear the Sergeant say the Ripper confessed to the murder of Terry Derry too? It seems the more murders he confesses to, that man, the better he sleeps at night.

Till the eve of my departure, then: I'll get you to drive me to the airport, I daren't rely on the trains.

No, that's all I'm taking with me, a single overnight bag as cabin luggage. I like to be first through customs. I can't stand hanging about Heathrow. When I get back, it's a different story, I can load up in Hong Kong, see? Up here for thinking, down here for delivering mail. Bloody old Orloff, I promised I'd get him a video cassette recorder. The money people once spent on stationery, they now spend on porno video movies. And MacLollard wants a dozen Japanese watch-games for his grandson, I don't know: one of these days I'm going to jack up. You should have seen Alick Sidebottom's face when I said I didn't think I'd be able to see his sister in Bournemouth. He walked straight out into a corner of his yard, and wouldn't even look at me. In the end, I relented; I suppose I'll have to make a special trip down from London. Murial Topwaite will have to meet me in Renfrew, there's no way I'll be getting to Oban.

Did you hear what they're doing at the PO? The most disgraceful thing ever you heard of. They're going to make Fargo and me sit for a competitive examination, and the one who gets the highest marks will keep the job as postal officer. Did you know the automatic exchange was invented by a Kansas City undertaker? He wouldn't have done it, if the girls hadn't kept diverting his death calls to rival undertakers. Yes, they've advertised our job on the counter. Thrown our job wide open, as though we didn't exist. Thirty-five years of postal service between us: I got away to a late start. We've both spoken to the union rep, but he says nothing can be done; every new postman in this nation is being made to sit for the exam, and from what Fargo's heard, it's very difficult. It takes two and a quarter hours. No one's passed it yet. You've got to view a host of little figures and guess which one doesn't belong, and for ten minutes they give you a hundred names of towns, in four groups, which you're supposed to memorize: names you never heard of, like 'Sackville West': then you're given a test in which you have to assign these towns to groups. I ask you. In another test, you have to tell, at a glance, if 'Dame Professor Melanie Mendelssohn-Beuve, 2B Cassowary Close, Mt Parnassus 6132' is the same address as 'Dame Professor Melanie Mendelssohn-Beuve, 2B Cassowary Close, Mt Parnassus 6312' and so forth. And they try to trip you up: you're handed a form, on which to write your name and application, but it's really a test. It says in the instructions 'do not use block letters'. I can't see myself beating Fargo, I've seen him doing crossword puzzles. He seemed pretty cocky when he told me about it, not as upset as I might have preferred.

Damn it, I won't give in without a fight! I'm going to study on the plane. If a customer tends a fifty-dollar note to buy five 7c stamps and three aerograms at 51c a piece, and a sheet of one hundred 22c stamps, at the same time offering for postage a parcel weighing 7.7k, at the rate of 10c per k for each k up to 5k, then 7c per 500g for every subsequent 500g up to 7.5k, then 12c per k or part thereof thereafter, how long will Tex be kept waiting, who's forgotten the key to his private box as always?

Here we are then. Don't wait for my flight. I'm sorry you couldn't make it, for your sake. I'll see you when I get back. Please don't forget to feed my cats and collect the Khaki Campbell eggs from under the Mexican pines. Should anything come up I ought to know, you can leave a message at Trafalgar Tours, or the Tara Hotel.

To the bitter end, then.

8

Thank God you're here. I wasn't sure anyone would be at the airport to collect me.

Come on now, cheer up, it's not the end of the world! I've still got my right arm, and that's the one I use to pick my nose and wipe my bum. Can you grab my suitcase? Go easy now; that's Orloff's video cassette recorder.

Yes, as you say, I'm looking pretty well, all things considered. My arm was amputated by the best neurosurgeon in Scotland, I was very fortunate. He did the job as though he were removing the hand from a modern Pakistani thief. There's all the difference in the world between having your arm lopped off, and having it amputated by a skilled surgeon. Mind you, I'm not claiming it didn't hurt. What's that you say? Haven't had your breakfast yet, I do apologize. I forgot what time it was, what time is it? I was wearing my watch on my left wrist, you see.

Well, what's been going on in young Dog Rock while I've been away? Mail been getting through all right? Aaron Cartwright's son in gaol: poor Aaron, he will be upset. No fault of Aaron's. Of course, I could see it coming, he was always a strange piece of work, that lad. I remember him coming up to me on the run once, with a peculiar look on his face. 'D'Arce,' he says, 'come here a minute.' He only wanted to squeeze my pimple, but I thought at the time, hello: there's something not quite right here. And now he's locked in a small room, with no freedom. It goes to show.

My word, it feels funny without the arm. I lost an old hatchet I'd had for years last March, and I can remember

148

thinking as I hunted for it – I kept looking for it in the same place, over and over, you know how you do – there's an intimation of mortality here, Lord D'Oliveres, in your being severed from this favoured object. When you've handled something every day for years, it comes as quite a wrench to lose it.

What are you doing? Where are we going? Don't say they finished the freeway?

They finished the freeway. So now we're less than two hours' drive from the city.

I got to London all right, and after a week moping about there and in Bournemouth, I went off on a Best of Britain coach. Rain! I should have guessed that, after such a warm summer, we'd have an early winter. Laying in the Strathclyde Infirmary, I did nothing but listen to rain. Were you aware Glasgow has a cool wet summer and a cold wet winter? I will say this for them there though, they made my stay very pleasant.

I won't bore you with the details of the first four days of my trip. You can get neck injuries on British high speed rail, trying to read the names of the stations, but you don't see much from the windows of a coach either, if it's pouring rain. The windows fog up on the inside; you're forever wiping them with the sleeves of your cardigan. Luckily for him, I was seated next to a man who spoke no English at all.

On the second night out we stayed at the Beaufort Hotel in Bath, so despite the rain, I set out for Weston, which is two miles from the abbey, just to set foot on the Cotswold Way, where it ends at the Primrose Hill kissing gate. There's a squeeze stile about 400 yards further on, and I walked as far as there. I've always finished up in Bath, but there's something to be said for starting in Bath, and keeping the weather behind you. I thought to myself, I could walk home from here in three days.

How I hate this modern world! You see people getting on the train in Bath and going to work in London. I like things on a walking scale; that's why I like Britain. You can't walk around Australia, there's too much of it and

149

it's too much the same. In defiance of the spirit of the YHA, the Dog Rock hostel has a car park.

I heard they're putting pinball machines in all the British hostels.

We stayed in Liverpool the third night. The rain had eased a little during the day, and so I took the opportunity of taking a walk, when we stopped for lunch at Ludlow to admire the famous Tudor inn there. What's the name of it? The Feathers, that's right. I must tell you about the interesting pet shop I found in Ludlow.

On day four we drove to the Lake District, or so it said on my brochure. Frankly, it could have been anywhere. The mist was down and rain was pouring.

It was on the fifth day my accident occurred, during inspection of the Moffat Woollen Mill. Earlier that day, I'd been bridegroom in a humourous mock wedding at Gretna Green, and whether this unsettled me I don't know, but I absolve the Woollen Mill from blame entirely. It was my own fault I got my hand caught in the carding machine, I should have been more careful. They did everything they could to free my arm, but I could see it was no use. In the end, I told the coach driver to drive on without me.

After my arm had been amputated – just below the elbow, though I guess with this lifelike prosthesis, you could easily think I was completely normal – I was taken to the Strathclyde Infirmary. A TT rep called by to visit me, and seemed relieved when I said I wouldn't sue.

I fully accept it was my own stupid fault; thankfully, the carding machine suffered no damage, and I'm told I'll get so fond of this prosthesis, I'll make a codicil to have it buried with me. I have to learn how to use it yet, of course, it's very modern. It can only be used on people who've had their arm amputated by a skilled neurosurgeon; something to do with the electrical resistance at the neuromuscular synapse.

You know I can't get it to move at all? In the end, I was referred to a psychiatrist, who said I was perfectly abnormal, and that once I recovered from the shock, they'd be watching out for me in street fights.

I hope he's right. I can bend three fingers and my thumb, with a bit of concentration, but my middle finger seems to have a mind of its own; it stays sticking up in the air.

Are the cats all right? I bought them a little something in Hong Kong, but lost it in quarantine. Good Lord, we're in Dog Rock already! What are those horrible signs everywhere? 'Black Wattle Country Estate', 'Misty Vista Estate', 'Natural Springs Estate'; you don't mean to say they're subdividing the old holding yards? Where's Jack to plant his turnips? And that big paddock under Broken Dream Boulevarde – fifty acre blocks at forty grand a block. I could have bought the whole main street for less, ten years back.

And why are they digging up the footpaths? How am I supposed to ride over all that wet clay to reach the boxes? Sewerage Scheme? What Sewerage Scheme? That's not an auction sign on Benjy's place, is it? Has Benjy died? I thought not, I can see his old Friesian housecow with her dairymeal sack coat. The selfish old bugger must have battleaxed his block. That's the only two-storey house he could afford, where does he propose to go? A man can't make cheese without a staircase; what's his cheese press to bite on?

Take me home, wait a bit: the Hobbit's shop is empty. You're not telling me the Hobbit's gone? Campbelltown, oh dear. Still, there won't be much feed for tethered animals, once the septics are empty. When a town's vacant blocks have disappeared, it becomes just another suburb. And where's a man to get firewood? I'll guarantee every brick veneer going up has a big wood-burning stove.

I'd like to have seen the PM's face when the Hobbit asked for a redirection form. He was our biggest customer, the only mail order business in town. I'll miss those heavy little letters, all full of coins, that came in every day. It's funny how letters with cheques disappear, while envelopes with coins are perfectly safe. All postal workers patch them carefully with PO tape, and send them on their way, though, strictly speaking, they're illegal. We're not monsters: I'd sooner collect ten Deutschmarks tax for the Luftwaffe, than jettison a kid's dream. He was most cooperative too, the Hobbit; always dispatched his outgoing orders on mail count day. By far our biggest customer for the large padded postal bookbags. Green teeth and blood capsules were his biggest lines, and they're easily broken. I'm glad I bought one of his poster-sized urgent telegrams for my lounge-room wall now. He was building up his horse lover line, how did he go bad?

Stop at the noticeboard, will you? That's the quickest way to read the yellow rain gauge.

A message from the Baha'i Faith, that'd be one of those Balthazars. Horse wanted, suitable pleasure riding, 14.3 to 15 hands. I could make a few suggestions there. Goat's milk for sale, I know who that'll be. Torana 1500, two-door manual, 47,000k, one owner – no thanks! Poppinjay Herbs, that's a new one; what's become of Lavender House? Nine hundred and fifty salmon face bricks, Mucklethwart's getting too big for his boots. Duck eggs, poor old Vince, he's convinced there's a market for Muscovy duck eggs. Dog Rock Beautification Committee Annual Dinner Dance, I won't be going to that. Bonny Tops High School uniform for sale, blouse 42" bust, it's about time they got rid of her, I blame her for last year's HSC fiasco. Hello, here's the draw of the Old Friend's raffle, dinner ticket pink F9, D'Arcy D'Oliveres! You might have told me.

Look at this: someone's nicked poor old Alick's garden gnome. And there's my kitchen setting for sale, formica and chrome, $80.

That's my telephone number.

Take me home immediately!

Well everything appears to be in the usual disorder, it must be someone's idea of a joke. A way to have me driven half mad by endless telephone inquiries. Come with me into the garden Maud, I'm keen to see if the spuds are up.

Just look at that. Nipped and withered by frost, like my heart, and chewed off, like my left arm. Someone's horse has been in this yard. Dog Rock is not the village it was. If the noticeboard suggests otherwise, it's only because the new chums don't use it.

I'm tired now, jetlag has hit. No hurry: I've still two weeks of leave in which to make a decision on my future.

What's the time? Three a.m.! You should have kept me talking till dark. If you can get through that first day, you're right, but I can never sleep on a jumbo. I had a toddler in the seat next to me on the way out, and she couldn't sleep either. The stay in Hong Kong's not much help, as you tend to stay awake all night, in a hotspot like Hong Kong.

There was never much to do in Dog Rock at 3 o'clock in the morning. I'll go down and talk to Dudley the baker. It's young Cartwright's girlfriend I'm sorry for! The pressure those prisoners exert on their girlfriends from inside the slammer is something to see.

Six o'clock, by George I'm grateful! He had me working the bread slicer, I was determined to do it too, but I was shaking, I don't mind telling you. It brought it all back, you see.

I will say it's amazing what you can do with one arm hanging loose. One chopstick's no good, but they'll give you a big wooden spoon, if you ask in Cantonese.

I want to go down and see Bert, in case he still wants to play bowls. He's up and about at 2 a.m., being an old dairyman. His father used to rise at 1.30 a.m.

Does the whole town know about my accident? I ask, because Dudley never mentioned it. They do? That's good, it saves me repeating myself, time and again.

'Bert! How's it going?'

'D'Arcy! I never thought I'd see your gardening shirt again, though I see you've removed the Australia Post tags, as required by regulation. And how can you wear shorts in this weather? Sit down and have two cups of tea.'

'Why did you think that, Bert?'

'Well, with one arm missing, like.'

'There's a good chance I'll regain the use of it, and even if I don't, I can still deliver mail. The modern postal motorcycle has no clutch.'

'Now listen, D'Arcy, supposing you lose that job anyway? What the hell are you going to do? An invalid pension won't buy much Tagamet. Wouldn't you be better off back home in Maggie Thatcher's England?'

'I don't accept there's nothing I can do, Bert, I've been giving the matter some thought. Derry's left a vacant niche, to give but one example. I know beekeeping's heavy work, but where there's a will, there must be a way. And how are things going with Mal and Cass?'

'I quit the job as manager. I said to him, you need someone who knows twice what I do about cattle, but only someone twice as stupid as me would be prepared to work for you. Did you hear he's been asked to judge the Brahmins at next year's Royal?'

'He was about to apply for a fettler's job when I left, do you know if he got it?'

'He can't lift a crowbar! Anyway, I don't speak to him, since he asked old Claude to do his tax return. You know that swimming pool she's putting in? That's officially a dam. I tell you, if I were a younger man with a sounder heart in my body . . . And where do you think you're going to put your bees? You won't get them into the park now.'

'I don't say I'll be beekeeping, Bert. Just thought I'd mention it in passing.'

That's the police car outside my hedge of Mexican pine. What have I done now?

'I can't let you drive your car, D'Arcy. You'll have to sit for a new licence.'

'That's all right, Sarge, I understand. You're only doing your duty.'

'I was very sorry to hear about your arm. Can you still play bowls do you think?'

'I don't know that I'll even be trying. When something like this happens to someone who lives as quiet a life as I do, it's a chance to break a few old habit patterns.

There's no use me pretending I'll be the same man as I was.'

'And how are you going to get around town, now that you can't drive?'

'I'll walk. Did you get the results of the autopsy?'

'The case is over, D'Arcy. It was all a misunderstanding. There was no involvement at this end. The Ripper built that implement himself, and designed it to look like nothing on earth. It's not clear why he did Derry in, but who can understand the motives of a man who wears his hair in pink spikes?'

'Who indeed. Did you get the results of the autopsy?'

'I can't see you breaking any habit patterns. And are you sure you can't play bowls? I thought we had a good chance of winning Country Week this year.'

'The reason I can't forget Derry, Sarge, I'm thinking of taking over his niche. I want to be a one-armed beekeeper. Will you do me a small favour? I want you to mention this ambition of mine, to every person you speak with.'

There's some crimson bottlebrush flowering by the Cow Flat Road, we might take a look at it this evening.

We'll go out at dusk every evening, and just keep standing there, dusk after dusk, by the side of the road, till something happens, and a move is made. I'm expecting a move to be made.

Off we go then, it's a lovely time of year: smell the native daphne? The sassafras by the pass is flowering; that's a beautiful sight. There goes Dion on his big Ducati Dharma, still in one piece I'm pleased to see. Alphonse the axeman; he supplies all the fencing timber hereabouts, won't touch a chainsaw. Someone coming up on foot now; Shane Hardacre, running in for football training at Bonny Tops oval, all the way from Barren Grounds. But surely, the football season must be over? He's doing some private training then. He runs in and out forty miles twice a week, during the football season. There'd be no fitter footballer in the district. He's captain of the district side. There's talk of him signing with a city club next year, and if he could survive, the crowds would love him. He's game as Ned Kelly, quicker than a ferret, with wonderful ball skills, but only eight stone, and I wonder really if that's big enough. If ever he did get caught in a tackle, he'd never play again.

There goes friend Hector, in his wretched Rent-a-Cock panel van. Someone's hired the little Silkie, I can see its stupid pompom head. Hector won't wave at me anymore: you'd think I'd put my calf on his cow.

The Funny Farm's been burnt to a shell: luckily, no one was home at the time. Brian O'Bastardbox will be pleased, he'll be free now to fell those massive pines that signify Dog Rock to ex-residents. He lives in terror of one of those pine trees falling on his house and crushing him to death. When the nor' westerly bushfire gales blow in summer, don't those pine trees roar. I hear the fire broke out on a night there was no wind at all.

That's where Fargo hit the wombat, setting the whole business in motion, and just round the corner is where it's going to end, and there goes Fargo himself, my rival, driving off to visit his sister in the Hudson, with Banjo taking the breeze.

What time do you make it? Five p.m. Here comes someone, yes, it's Bert, driving Van Effendonk's ancient truck. He turned up the firetrail, this is it then: get out of sight and don't be alarmed.

'What are you doing here, D'Arcy? Does anyone know you're about? If you're looking for blooms, I'll show you some beauties up the track.'

'What's the wheelbrace for, Bert? Expecting a flat tyre?'

'I was wondering if you'd mind checking the tension on some of these wheelnuts for me. One of the left-side wheels is loose, and I left my Declinax at home.'

'Do you think I can do it with one arm?'

'I shouldn't be at all surprised. I hate to ask, D'Arcy, but you know what he's like. If his truck was damaged, God help me.'

'God help you anyway, Bert. Give me the wheelbrace then.'

'I thought you couldn't work your new arm?'

'I'm still using the two I was born with, see?'

'What th...? What's going on? You haven't lost an arm at all!'

'No, this is just a bit of moulded plastic, expertly applied.'

'I don't understand.'

'Oh yes you do. You're in my way, Bert. There's no room in Dog Rock for the two of us. You thought you'd come out here to bump me off, but I'm going to bump you off instead.'

'You're mad.'

'Stand back, I'm warning you!'

'You won't kill me, you wouldn't have it in you.'

'Who do you think killed Derry then?'

'Derry? He died a natural death.'

'Aha! Thank you. That's what I was waiting to hear. Derry was supposed to have been murdered by the Ripper, Bert. Or had you forgotten?'

'Get out of my way, D'Arcy. I'm driving back to town.'

'Keep away from the cabin of that truck, or I'll drop you where you stand! You're looking at a man who's lobbed a few parcels into sagging mailbags in his time. I'm a dead shot.'

'What do you want from me?'

'A full confession.'

'You won't get that. You can't prove a thing boy, or you wouldn't have shown your hand. I've been onto you, all along.'

'And I've been doing a bit of thinking, would you care to hear what I think? The Ripper's first murder occurred on Tuesday, May 29th, when you had the perfect alibi: you were sitting, with a coach full of people, including your long-suffering wife, on the other side of the world, being ferried from Wroxton, the showplace Cotswold village, to Blenheim Palace, birthplace of the famous commoner, Sir Winston Churchill, on Day Twelve of a Best of Britain Trafalgar Tour, that left London on May 18th, a Friday. Now I'm perfectly prepared to believe that at this stage, you were no more than a disgruntled dairyman.'

'Rave on.'

'I intend to. How would you have known of this murder, I asked myself. And of course, the answer was simple: before starting your Traditional Europe Tour, which left London on June 3rd, a Sunday, you spent four nights in London, three of them under the TT three-night package at the Tara Hotel, Kensington. Now what is the first thing a retired Australian dairyman does, when he finds himself with free time in London? I put it to you, he goes straight to Australia House, to read the paper. I know you dealt with the Commonwealth Bank next door; Miss Kareer told me.'

'You low, sneaking, prying worm. So you've spoken to Miss Kareer?'

'Where do you think I buy my own tickets? The Ripper's first murder, being as the victim was a Labor MP, received a lot of coverage. I have ascertained it was front-page news in every Australian morning paper of Wednesday May 30th, so even if you had to be content with a *Courier Mail* or *Mercury*, you'd have seen it.'

'As if I'd read a *Courier Mail*!'

'But you did something else in London, that very few Australians do. You caught the tube to Bethnal Green, and not to visit the doll museum.'

'How do you know?'

'I'm just guessing. It's a great city, London, isn't it Bert? It's amazing the shops you can find there. What about that shop near Berkeley Square that sells antique scientific instruments? There can't be much demand for them, surely. Probably only enough for one such shop to exist, in the entire world.'

'What are you driving at?'

'I'll admit I was confused back there for a while, nothing seemed to be making sense. But once Derry's body was dug up, everything promptly fell into place.'

'Did it now.'

'The police didn't seem much concerned when they found only one of Derry's arms. I presume they thought a wild dog had been busy. It was clever of you to have dismembered and buried the body, especially as you didn't kill him.'

'As if I'd kill Derry!'

'You must have received a few nasty stings, lugging those hives about, but they wouldn't have bothered you, would they Bert, because you're immune to stings. I thought at first it couldn't have been you dropped that hive in Miss Hathaway's stables, because I could tell you'd never worked bees, and yet I could see you had not been stung, when I visited you the next day. Of course, I didn't realize then, that you and Derry were great mates as boys, and I guess it was hardly possible to visit him, without getting stung.'

'I don't know what you're talking about.'

'As soon as I realized Derry must have lost that arm in the war – and that's why he'd never show his face here again, he couldn't bear the thought of keeping goal – I got to wondering how he managed to work his bees with only one arm. It's hard enough with two, at times. Something seemed to sound an alarm. Perhaps an ad I'd read once, in a beekeeping journal back home. When I got to London Bert, you know the second thing I did? I looked up the bee-supply houses in the phone book, and what do you think I found? A little shop, above some stairs, in the shabby suburb of Bethnal Green, specializing in the sale and manufacture of equipment for the one-armed bee-keeper.'

'Huh!'

'I had a photo of you with me; that one from last year's *Post*, where you're accepting, tongue in cheek as I recall, a prize for drawing the best freehand map of Australia. It was confirmed you had visited the shop, sometime early in May, to express, on behalf of a client – one Mr Terrence Derry by name – complete satisfaction, with what is described in the catalogue as "the all-purpose prosthesis for the professional one-armed bee-keeper".'

'I don't have to listen to this!'

'I had, as you see, some parts of the puzzle, though the principal piece eluded me. Who could have given you the idea of smuggling swamp parrots out of Australia? I'm pretty sure I never mentioned I'd heard that parrot to you, and if I had, it would not have been in economic terms. Though Derry must have known of the bird, I feel reasonably certain there was nothing sinister in your relationship with him, beyond a natural desire on your part to protect his privacy, and a natural desire on his, to inculcate on you his doctrinaire social-insect political theories. Otherwise, you could hardly have done the things you have done, this last six months.'

'You've no proof of what I've done. You're just bluffing.'

'In order to determine your contact, and to try to understand your motives, I had to do as you would do. I put myself in your gumboots, as a first-time Australian tourist to Europe. I took the tour that you took, and stopped at the places you stopped at. I prowled around Salisbury, Exeter and Plymouth, Polperro, Wells and Bath, hardly knowing what I was looking for, until, in Ludlow, acting on a hunch, I wandered into the new town, in among the council houses, and far from the Tudor tourist trap. I don't know why I did it: perhaps I felt a slight reaction could have set in by this stage. In any event, I found the shop.'

'You found the shop. Why don't you admit you listened on the line, when he rang me that time at home?'

'Because I never listen to phone calls, Bert: I don't even make free calls. So that's why you felt you had to get rid of me?'

'I never liked you from the beginning. You're a stuck-up Pommy mongrel.'

'You thought I was a smuggler.'

'I don't doubt you are!'

'You'll have to take my word I'm not. So I found the pet shop, with the two big stuffed crimson rosellas in the window, and I went inside, as you would have done, to boast that I came from where they fly free. And after asking me how I could wear shorts in such weather – I replied it was because I was Australian – the proprietor got out his map of Australia, and jokingly asked if I came from anywhere near the Dog Rock National Park. And then he asked if I'd like to make some money, and he showed me the list of names he showed you, and I just had time to tell him they were both dead, before I realized I'd have to run back to The Feathers, if I wanted to catch the coach.'

'What did you think of the Ludlow dairy market?'

'I don't remember it, offhand. Why did you kill both Milligan and Evans?'

'For the same reason I'm killing you. Don't move, D'Arcy. This is a derringer. You've never worked as hard as me. *No* one's worked as hard as me, and what have I got to show for it?'

'You'll get your reward in the next life, Bert.'

'I'm not waiting till then. Milligan and Evans were parrot smugglers: he didn't give me your name, but I figured you were in it too.'

'And you thought you'd be able to drive me out, without actually killing me.'

'Your job's as good as gone, son. Dead men don't deliver mail.'

'How will you explain the bullet in my breast?'

'This gun won't leave much of a hole. You'll be the victim of a hit-and-run accident.'

'As you had planned all along.'

'Move, D'Arcy! Let's get out of sight of the road.'

'Why did you try to implicate Derry, by using Derry's prosthesis?'

'I didn't mean to implicate him. He left it with me every winter. I figured no one would know what it was. The first killing was done with a corkscrew. That's what gave me the idea.'

'But you lost it.'

'That's right.'

'So you had to go back to Britain in a hurry, or Derry wouldn't be able to work his bees. You couldn't even wait for advance purchase fares. But they hadn't another implement in stock, so you asked to have one made up.'

'That's right.'

'Then, when you turned up to collect the thing, they'd found one, and mailed it, while you were in Scotland.'

'That's right. Stand by this tree. Put your hands behind your head.'

'I'd rather cover my eyes, thanks.'

'Suit yourself and say your prayers.'

'That was the night, late in August, you roared all through *The Mousetrap*. Then you flew home. And when you got home, Derry had died. You could have pinned it on him, why didn't you?'

'Because he was my friend. The last job I did was for him. Or rather, the second last job. Ready?'

'Just a bit: let me die easy. Evans and Milligan I can understand, and Rubyfruit Rocqueforte you've just explained, and Morgan was doing those margarine commercials, but what about Mr Justice Bolch-Corio?'

'He was my reaction to Mr Justice Safehouse ruining my chainsaw. You know what they cost to replace? Safehouse is a poser. When he has guests in, he floats in a dozen Charolais from the Icechest Brothers, just to look good in his paddocks. Back they go on the Monday. I knew as soon as I seen 'em, they'd come straight off a float. All scouring, in midwinter – does he think we're stupid or something?'

'And about that implement. I delivered it to you in the mail. You had no hold notice lodged, so I presume a Balthazar collected it. I recall the casing it came in distinctly. But you didn't want it by that stage. So guessing that Fargo would deliver parcels to me but not to yourself, and hardly game to hand it in over the counter *refused by addressee*, you put my name on it, ridding yourself of incriminating evidence while implicating me at the same time. You rigged that accident, using a wombat you'd found by the side of the road, and placed the parcel where you knew Fargo would come to grief when he hit the wombat. But you didn't reckon on that cattle dog chewing off the address.'

'That's right.'

'And as to shutter 63: Balthazars aside, Dudley and you are the only two people awake in this town at 2 a.m. on a Monday. It had to be one of you fiddling all night with that cable and making me cranky. The shutter first fell on the night you returned from Scotland. So you were the likelier suspect, seeing as how the cable runs right past your back door.'

'Yes, and I *still* haven't got the phone on! All right, you've said enough.'

Bang!

As I'd hoped, I dropped my arm, and deflected the bullet from the plastic moulding. Run! I don't know how many shots he has left, but he won't waste them in the dark.

Ow! My crook knee again! I've twisted it down this wombat burrow.

'Ha ha, I heard that, D'Arcy! And now I'm coming in for the kill . . .'

I can hardly walk and a wombat's coming. Wait a bit! I've an idea! What's the time? Six thirty p.m. Fargo will be back this way shortly.

'There's only one way out of here, D'Arcy, for a man with a gammy leg!'

He'll be waiting for me by that culvert. We'll know when he's close, from his pacemaker. He's got a heavy-duty model. When I went out to pick flowers with him once, I kept looking round for kangaroos. Now: when this wombat gets close, I'll grab one end and you grab the other. They're deaf as posts and thick as a brick. Got it? Take no notice of the creature's heavy breathing, that's an attempt to frighten us.

Is that Fargo? Is that the Hudson I hear coming? He's like a riding-school horse, Fargo, he comes back quicker than he goes out – it *is* Fargo! Quick then! No time to lose! When the Hudson hits the corner, chase the wombat onto the road and run. It's a long shot, but it just might work: if he rolls it, he'll roll it down the culvert. What you must remember, there's not a front end for that vehicle in the whole of this country.

Now!

He did it. He saw the wombat and rolled the car on top of Bert. Fargo's out cold and so's Banjo, but what about Bert? Is he still alive?

'D'Arcy: do you forgive me?'

'Of course I forgive you, Bert.'

'I never killed Derry.'

'I know you didn't.'

'Derry was my best friend. I only got rid of some social parasites that had no business being alive. I've had a very hard life, D'Arcy: my missus has had a lot to put up with. When I saw the wealth of those Common Market dairy farmers, something snapped inside me.'

'I understand, Bert, and rest assured I won't breathe a word of this to anyone. Who knows but I wouldn't have done the same thing, if I'd been in your position? I'll tell the copper we were looking at some flowers, and you were killed in an accident. Let that spiky-headed guilt-ridden city hoodlum take the credit, if that's what he wants.'

'Thank you, D'Arcy.'

'Not at all, Bert. Now I'll just tread on your chest, to make it quicker for you.'

9

I've regained full use of the arm. They found the old one, posted it out, and Opfinger sewed it back on.

I'm sorry I had to tell you an untruth, but I wanted Renee, Carmel & Co to spread the untruth around town. I never lost the arm at all, but I'll have to behave, for the rest of my stay in Dog Rock, as if I had. It's worth it, to protect Bert's reputation.

Tonight is the night of Fargo's presentation, and all the town will be there, from fencing contractors in their Valiant Chargers, to the new settlers in their Volvo station sedans. He is to be presented with the silver medal of the RSPCA – that's the Royal Society for the Prevention of Cruelty to Animals, in case you didn't know. When Miss Hathaway heard how he rolled his car, rather than hit that wombat, and knowing how much his vehicle means to him – he speaks of little else – she got straight on to the RSPCA and arranged tonight's presentation.

Of course, being a shy, modest sort of man, Fargo at first wanted nothing to do with it, but the more he demurred the more insistent she became, until at last the PM, stepping in and speaking of public relations, arranged for the presence of the press there tonight, and there's to be a dignitary from Australia Post, as well as the local mayor and all the councillors, and Fargo's to wear his postman's uniform, and to give a short speech on how postmen love animals. All of which has been a great blow to my own prospects of retaining the position, but I won't be thinking of those tonight, as supper will be served immediately afterwards, and I hear Boronia Lilywhite has been baking her famous cakes all week, as she loves God's creatures dearly.

Have you seen the hall? As you will note from the foundation stone, it was opened on September 9, 1931 by the Honourable S.S. Belfast, MLA, Minister for Labour and Industry, whose daughter, I understand, has been invited to attend tonight's function. It's a red-brick building, with an iron roof, so let's hope we don't get a hailstorm during Fargo's acceptance speech. I must admit the hall is seldom used nowdays, except for the annual P&C Dance, and the monthly meetings of the Dog Rock Community Development Association, which are poorly attended. Brian O'Bastardbox conducts art classes here, and indoor basketball is played weekly, while other activities include jazz ballet, karate, housie, and donation of blood. The flagpole and the five chrome horns of the defunct PA are never used. The rising sun over the podium, above the motto '1914-18' hints at former duty as a rissole, and not, as might be thought, a Japanese field canteen.

It seems Bert *did* have an accomplice: the Sarge chased a black Chevy Corvette all the way to Barren Grounds yesterday, where, luckily, the road gang was digging up the road, forcing the Chevy to stop. The man driving it was a Turk, who spoke not a word of English. The Sergeant took him back to the station, and charged him, using the Turkish bail form.

Seven thirty, we'd better go in. All the kids are here. Bryony Belvedere's brought that blessed brat of hers, we'll steer clear of the Belvedere clan. The louts are slouching on trestles up the back, waiting for the girls to walk by. No, not that row: Mrs Orloff! This will do us nicely; conveniently close to the table with the cakes.

Is that the PM looking for me? It is, too. He must want someone to tap the microphone, and I'm still wearing uniform. Haven't had time to get changed.

'Sambo wants a word backstage, D'Arce. See if you can't calm him down.'

Poor Sambo, he must be in a dreadful state, but Serepax, at this stage, could do more harm than good. Did you notice D'Oilycart in the front row? I wouldn't mind betting he intends giving Sambo the hard eye all night, as if to say, 'I know the truth'.

'Come on Sambo, calm yourself down. When the stage lights are on, you won't see them. Just think of them as Telecom subs, with letterboxes of poor design.'

'It's not that, D'Arce. I just asked the PM about our exam. We're not the only candidates.'

'What do you mean? Who else is there?'

'Dr Isbester is sitting for it too.'

'But he hasn't got a motorcycle licence!'

I will sell my car and leave this town at 4 a.m. one moon-less night, so I won't be able to look behind me or listen to the birds. I will walk as far as Plymouth and catch the train from there.

Somewhere in the world another town awaits me, a smaller town than Dog Rock.

I will go there, and work as a postman.

Also by David Foster

PLUMBUM

A novel

Australia and New Zealand proudly presents the world's most notorious rock band!

Featuring the unbelievably beautiful and confused SHARON SCOTT on vocals. The unbelievably handsome and romantic JASON BLACKMAN on lead guitar. The unbelievably fat and materialistic ROLAND ROCCA on keyboards. The unbelievably powerful and insensitive FELIX FARQUAHAR on drums. The unbelievably intelligent and cynical PETE BLACKMAN on bass.

The ultimate heavy metal experience.

MORE ABOUT PENGUINS AND PELICANS

For further information about books available from Penguin please write to Dept EP, Penguin Books Ltd, Harmondsworth, Middlesex UB7 ODA.

In the U.S.A.: For a complete list of books available from Penguin in the United States write to Dept DG, Penguin Books, 299 Murray Hill Parkway, East Rutherford, New Jersey 07073.

In Canada: For a complete list of books available from Penguin in Canada write to Penguin Books Canada Ltd, 2801 John Street, Markham, Ontario L3R 1B4.

In Australia: For a complete list of books available from Penguin in Australia write to the Marketing Department, Penguin Books Australia Ltd, P.O. Box 257, Ringwood, Victoria 3134.

In New Zealand: For a complete list of books available from Penguin in New Zealand write to the Marketing Department, Penguin Books (N.Z.) Ltd, Private Bag, Takapuna, Auckland 9.